SEAL in Charge
Silver SEALs Book 4

DONNA MICHAELS

*New York Times & USA Today
Bestselling Author*

About this Book

She's the only one to get past his guard. He's the only one to break down her walls.

For nearly thirty years, retired US Navy SEAL Commander Archer Malone made the Navy his home. Now he's out and tasked by a DHS Secret Division Command to lead a hand-picked civilian team. Their mission: locate and eliminate a rogue crew chatter indicates intends to target Wall Street.

The problem: no one knows what they look like, or if they plan to rob or bomb the Federal Reserve Bank of New York.

The bigger problem: one of his team members is the attractive—off limits—single mother of a Navy SEAL he once commanded.

Sandy Vickers is as good at blending in as she is at locating people. A skill she honed working for the D.A.'s office while her son was young, then for DHS after he joined the Navy. Proud of him for following in his late father's footsteps and serving the country, she jumps at the chance to do her part too when offered a spot on a secret DHS team. Too bad the SEAL in charge is her son's sexy former commander…the one who always leap*frog*'d her pulse.

Forced proximity soon snaps their control, and they give in to their attraction. But when their location is attacked, Archer realizes the economy isn't the only thing threatened with destabilization. Now their lives—and hearts—are on the line, and this silver SEAL is determined to keep Sandy safe, unmask and hunt down the traitor, and take out the rogue crew…before they all run out of time.

SEAL in Charge is connected to my Dangerous Curves Series. All my books are written as stand-alones, so there is no need to read the series, But I recommend checking them out if you enjoy the environment. The same goes for the Silver SEALs books, too.

Thanks for reading,

~Donna
www.donnamichaelsauthor.com

DEDICATION

A huge thank you to all the amazing Suspense Sisters. Once again, I'm honored to be your 'sister', and am excited to create a SEAL to let loose in this world!

And to a very special member of my street team, Sandy Davidson Scheer, whom I named the heroine after in this story. I truly appreciate all you do for me, so this one's for you, Sandy! ♥

♥

.

CHAPTER ONE

Deep blues and dark purple bleeding into orange and yellow with dawn, haloed the bright orange sphere as it appeared to slowly rise out of the ocean.

There was nothing like an East Coast sunrise.

Archer Malone, U.S. Navy SEAL Commander, (Ret.), had witnessed them all over the world. Some were more vibrant, some more colorful, but none took his breath quite like the ones he'd had the privilege of witnessing from this back deck since he was in diapers.

He shifted the large Adirondack chair holding his two-hundred-five-pound frame, to meet the vista head on. Coffee steamed in the mug from which he sipped, while the sound of waves slapping the shore before receding to do it all over again hit his ears.

Serene. Peaceful. Heaven.

His little slice of heaven.

A well-earned slice. He'd given Uncle Sam twenty-eight years, twenty-seven of them as a Navy SEAL. Been sliced, shot, battered, bruised and broken, all for the country he loved. The last injury—he rotated his right shoulder and grimaced—got him booted. So, he'd returned to his favorite place.

The small N.J. cottage on Brigantine Beach had been in his family for decades. Many fond memories of spending weekends and a majority of summers here with his parents and older brother had kept him going while trying to survive in some of the world's worst shitholes, dealing with the darker side of humanity.

Those days were gone. So was most of his family.

No one left but his mother now. Born and raised in Queens, she was a New Yorker through and through. He knew that although she used to love the shore, the memories surrounding this place were too hard for her to bear.

Not for him. They were exactly why he'd taken it off her hands seventeen years ago. His father had worked odd side jobs when not on shift at the fire station just to afford this place. No way was Archer going to sell his dad's dream. His father's blood, sweat, and tears.

It was his house now.

His home.

Over the past seven months, since Uncle Sam no longer had any use for him, Archer gave his time and muscle to fixing up the place. The house had been sitting vacant since he'd purchased it and had been in dire need of repairs. He set his mug on a side table then jogged down to the shore before he turned to eye his handiwork.

The new roof and fresh coat of weatherproof paint made a huge difference to curb appeal. Working on the house had been cathartic, just like his morning jogs. He pivoted and headed south, adopting a fast, steady pace. The cool morning air and fresh ocean breeze clung to him as he ran two miles down and two miles back to complete his four mile morning run.

Panting, wet, and invigorated, he grabbed his mug and removed a key from the side pocket of his sweats to unlock the floor-to-ceiling sliding glass doors before slipping the key back in his pocket. Nothing like starting off the day with a brisk run after watching a beautiful sunrise.

Once inside, he rinsed his cup in the sink of the kitchen he'd updated with high oak cabinets, stainless steel appliances, subway tiled backsplash, and granite countertops, as well as a small island snack bar.

It was open now. Not cramped. He wasn't a fan of cramped spaces.

Yanking his T-shirt over his head, he walked to the bathroom, removing the keys from his pocket before tossing his clothes into the hamper. His bathroom was now bigger, too. He stepped into the large walk-in shower he'd added by tearing down the wall to the small, adjacent bedroom, and considered all he'd done to the place. Even though the bungalow only had two bedrooms now, the updates inside brought the place out of the eighties and into the twenty-first century.

Done with his shower, he got dressed to head down to the marina. Archer always knew he wasn't an idle person but had thought perhaps retirement would slow him down a little. Kind of a "smell the roses" type of thing. Negative. He was a doer. Had to keep his hands busy. So, after renovating the house inside and out, he went stir crazy. He was a man of action, not inaction.

Thankfully, his old SEAL buddy, Jameson Knight, owner of the Knight Agency, threw a few bodyguard and security detail jobs his way. But when there weren't any assignments to keep his marksmanship sharp, or challenges for his physical abilities…boredom would set in.

So, he'd bought a boat.

The one he used to fantasize about while on missions overseas. He always knew that if he didn't die over in the sandbox, when he retired, he wanted a boat. But not just any boat.

A beautiful Pursuit OS Fishing Boat with its own bathroom, bedroom, and tiny kitchen. Great for when he'd needed to escape from the world.

Like now.

He parked his truck and headed down the dock to his slip. Only two years old, his boat—Liberty— didn't require much maintenance. Just routine inspection. Today, he was going to check the hull for corrosion above the water. Yesterday, he'd checked below.

Starting at the bow, he dropped to his knees, slowly working his way aft, utilizing the sun to help on the starboard side.

The sound of a sure-footed approach met his ears, and although the footsteps were practically silent, he estimated them to belong to a large male, over two-hundred-twenty-pounds. Couldn't be for him, though. He wasn't expecting visitors. Hell, he never got company, and that was just the way he liked it. Must be for the chartered fishing boat in the slip at the end of the dock.

When a pair of expensive, shiny, un-scuffed loafers came into his peripheral view and stopped, he returned his attention back to his chore. All right, so not for the fishing boat, but whatever the guy was selling, he wasn't buying.

"You're blocking the light." He refrained from adding "asshole." That was yet to be determined.

"That's the idea." The deep, very familiar voice had him immediately straightening.

"Crash?" He shot to his feet and turned to properly greet one of his former SEAL buddies. "Good to see ya, you son-of-a-bitch," he said, deploying the old hand-shake-shoulder-bump maneuver, grimacing slightly as pain rippled down his arm, chest, and back, reminding him why he was in Jersey instead of on a base in Virginia with his team...his former team.

"Good to see you, too, Archer."

Releasing his buddy, he stepped back and scowled at the guy's attire. A well-fitting black monkey suit, white shirt, black tie, and dark sunglasses. "Ah, hell. The rumors *are* true. You've

5

been assimilated. Man, I never thought I'd see the day you traded in your uniform for bureaucratic duds and a pencil-pushing government job."

His friend folded his arms across his chest and cocked his head. "And I never thought you'd ever retire out of the Navy."

Archer's scowl deepened to tighten his face. "Wasn't by choice," he grumbled, smacking his left palm off his right shoulder. "Taking a round last year, saving some rich politician's spoiled kid, earned me a one-way ticket out." He'd received a pat on the back from Uncle Sam, a medical discharge with no chance to contest and nothing— not even a thank you from the ungrateful brat.

He still had the use of his arm and eighty-five-percent of his strength but it wasn't enough. Not when a-hundred-and-ten was required.

"Well, the rumors about me are true," Crash said, changing the subject, wisely knowing Archer wasn't the type to look for pity. "So, no more call signs or rank. I'm just Silas or Si now. And I can assure you, I don't push a single goddamn pencil in my position at DHS."

Navy SEAL Silas Branson and his famous joyride escapade during BUD/S would always be *Crash* to him. But he sensed a serious undertone to his old friend's demeanor, so he kept that to himself and nodded instead.

"Which is why I'm here." Si removed his sunglasses and waved them at Archer's shoulder. "Can you still shoot?"

He stiffened, aggravation pinching his shoulders. Retired didn't mean dead. Or useless. "Fuck yeah, I can still out-shoot any of you yahoos. You know as well as I do the Navy trained us to shoot accurately with either hand. So now my left is my lead hand." He halted his rant as a slight grin tugged Si's lips. "You son-of-a-bitch. You knew all of that, so why are you egging me on?"

"Just wanted to see if the Archer Malone spark was still in existence."

He snorted. "It existed well before you were born, boy."

Si lifted a brow. "Then you were one hell of an eight-year-old."

"Damn straight."

They both laughed, and he used the time to really assess the man before him.

Silas had changed, but the loss of a son would change any man. Archer had been with him when he'd gotten the call, and although he knew that loss on a smaller scale, he couldn't even begin to imagine the depth of the pain the man carried.

Lines around his eyes and mouth were visible but not quite as deep as Archer's, and a few streaks of gray peppered Silas' black hair—the exact opposite of the black hair peppering his gray.

"How's Maggie? I heard you two got remarried." Archer had always liked her. She was meant for Silas. Grounded him as only a good woman could.

A smile spread across the guy's face and chased the shadows from his eyes. "Yeah, we did. And she's good. She's pregnant."

"No shit?" His brows shot up, and happiness made a long overdue appearance. "That's wonderful, man." He extended his hand for another shake, this time, with a shoulder slap. "Congratulations!"

A long time ago, he'd felt the elation he saw on his buddy's face. Then helpless, complete and total devastation, and fury when he'd discovered his girlfriend at the time had an abortion while he'd been on a mission. He understood it was the woman's body, but he was the father and hadn't been given a choice. It fucking sucked.

Those feelings stayed with him, and always would, but now wasn't the time to dwell. He had a bottle of JD at home to help drown his sorrows when needed. The chance of him ever having a child now were slim to none. Right now, though, it was about his friend, who truly deserved this joy.

"Do you know if it's a boy or a girl?" He released him and stepped back.

"A girl."

"Well, no offense, man, but I hope to hell she looks like your wife," he joked. "Maggie's a lot prettier than you."

Silas laughed. "Roger that."

Archer scratched the bridge of his nose then re-crossed his arms over his chest. "It's been nice catching up and shooting the shit and all, but I think it's time you told me why you're really here."

Shoving the glasses back on his suddenly serious face, Silas straightened his six foot three frame. "That conversation needs to be held in private."

He unfolded his arms and nodded to the ocean behind him. "We've got the whole Atlantic at our disposal." Without waiting for a reply, he gathered his stuff, boarded his boat, and stared down at the man. "Unhook the moor...or are you afraid to get your pretty suit wet?"

Silas flashed him the middle finger before removing the line and climbing on board.

Archer was still grinning when he started the engine and piloted them out to open ocean. Ten minutes later, he glanced to his silent passenger standing next to him, gripping the rail that bordered the ceiling of the cockpit. "This good enough?" he asked.

At Silas' nod, Archer cut the engine, secured two beers from the fridge nearby, and handed one to Mr. DHS. "Go on," he said, popping the cap on his longneck. "Pitch whatever it is you've come to pitch."

"What are your thoughts on robbing the Federal Reserve in New York?"

That immediately dislodged the beer sliding down his throat. He coughed and smacked his chest. "Look, man, I spent most of my savings on this beauty." He caressed his boat. "But if you need money, I can probably scrape some up for you. No need to get drastic."

"Appreciate the offer." Silas held up his free hand, a slight twitch to his lips. "But I was talking hypothetically. Could someone do it?"

"Oh." Archer took another swig of beer and shrugged. "Sure, I guess. Robbing is the easy part, it's getting out that could prove tricky. Why? Has there been chatter?"

"Yes, involving the FRB." Silas flipped the cap off his longneck and finally took a pull.

Archer waited for the man to continue, because his sixth sense told him there was most definitely more. And the sinking feeling in his stomach told him he was not going to like it. But after silence stretched for over thirty seconds, he raised a brow. "And why are you telling me instead of the F.B.I.?"

"Because we don't know if this impending threat is to rob it or blow it up."

Shit.

Unlike his firefighting father and brother, Archer had lived through the last time someone leveled a building in the city in which he grew up. He'd been home on leave, visiting his family in the Big Apple on 9/11, and scars from the gut-crushing massacre of that day never left him.

"You in?"

"Oh, hell, yeah. I'm in." There would not be another massacre in NYC.

Not on his watch.

Silas gave a curt nod. "You can put together a team, as big or as small as you want, to uncover the identity of these rogue bastards and take them down."

"Done." He already had two former military locals in mind. They worked out of Atlantic City for the Knight Agency, run by his former SEAL buddy, Jameson Knight.

"Good, because there's someone from DHS that I want on the team. She works out of our New York office, and is one hell of an investigator/analyst. She used to work for the D.A." Silas was staring at him as if waiting for a reaction.

"Okay...if you're recommending her, then she's got to be good." The hair on the back of his neck stood up. He narrowed his eyes. "Why do I get the feeling there's something you've yet to tell me?"

"She's a Navy SEAL mom, so I'm glad you're going to take point on this mission, because I can trust you to protect her."

Mother of a SEAL...

His mind immediately jumped to a mother of a froglet under his command three years ago. A widow with honey blonde hair, bright blue eyes, warm smile, great wit...he'd felt an instant connection, and intentionally kept his distance.

In all his years in the Navy, she was the only *family of the team* to ever spark his interest. Other than hearing she was a widow, he'd intentionally gone out of his way *not* to find out anything else about her. Christ, his attraction to the woman and the fact she was single turned her twice as dangerous, so he'd made damn sure they were never alone whenever she came down to Virginia to visit her son.

It hadn't stopped his attraction, but it had stopped him from acting on it.

No reason to even think about her now. This wasn't her. There were plenty of SEAL mothers out there.

Still, that sinking feeling in the pit of Archer's stomach grew larger. "Who is she?"

"Sandy Vickers."

Son-of-a-fucking-bitch...it *was* her.

CHAPTER TWO

Archer did his best to hold his reaction in check, despite the uptick in his pulse. He'd just agreed to work closely with a woman he was attracted to—who was also the mother of one of his former SEALs. A woman whose gaze had held interest whenever she'd looked at him. Damn...that was more than double trouble. It was a triple threat...unless, perhaps she'd remarried since he'd retired and been out of the loop. That was a line he'd never cross.

If she had a husband, he'd have no problem being around the beauty, other than dealing with the tightening going on in his chest at the thought of another man with the woman who starred in his secret fantasies. The one with the ability to disrupt his heartbeat with her mere presence. At the moment, though, none of that mattered.

Since Archer knew Silas was aware of the last team of SEALs he'd commanded, he lifted a brow and kept his emotions out of it. "Sandy Vickers? My froglet—Brian Vickers' mom?"

Silas nodded. "It's one of the reasons I chose you to lead this mission. I knew you'd want to have his six. Well...his mother's six."

Refusing to allow his mind or body to think about having Sandy's delectable six, he nodded and changed the focus. "Let's circle back to the subject of the F.B.I."

"A'ight."

"The threat of a bomb or theft at the Federal Reserve Bank still falls under their jurisdiction," he said. "They aren't going to try to get in my lane, are they?"

The last thing he needed was to step on government toes or to have his own stepped on. He washed away the bitter taste that thought left in his mouth with the last of his beer.

Silas shook his head. "They won't be involved at all. DHS got the green light to run this operation through me because chatter also suggests the possibility that the threat could be from the same ghost, rogue bastards responsible for the Munich bombings five years ago."

Archer stiffened, and his heart rocked in his chest as images of the carnage and destruction of that fateful October afternoon flashed through his head. He could still hear sirens and wailing, see the mangled bodies of the innocent tourists buried beneath rubble and debris from a brew house and a museum bombed by a jihad faction before his team and Silas' team had arrived. The SEALs had been sent in too late to stop the terrorists and save the hostages, and to this day, no one knew what the people responsible looked like. The group had knocked out surveillance cameras around the area and walked in and out without witnesses.

"So, if it is them," Silas continued, "I want someone in charge who understands what they're capable of and won't underestimate the threat."

Archer nodded, tossing his empty bottle in the nearby trash bin. "Roger that." Those bastards won't slip away again.

"But it isn't confirmed the chatter is from them," Silas said. "Let's head back." He pointed toward shore with his bottle. "We have an appointment with Ms. Vickers at her office in ninety minutes to see if she's uncovered anything else since my video conference with her yesterday."

A ripple infiltrated Archer's pulse.

There was so much wrong with that unsettling statement, he didn't know where to start. The fact Silas referred to Sandy as Ms. Vickers meant she had not remarried. He ignored the relief rushing through his body. That was a danger he had to avoid.

He cocked his head and raised a brow again. "You were that sure I'd say yes?"

A slight smile tugged the man's lips while he lifted a shoulder. "Absolutely."

Branson always was a good judge of people. But his travel time estimate was a little off.

"You'll have to call her and tell her we're going to be late," he said. "There's no way we can drive to New York City in less than two and a half hours."

Especially with midday traffic.

Now Silas cocked his head and raised a brow. "Who said we were driving?"

A grin tugged his lips. "Hooyah! I like the way you do business."

Although, now, it meant he had less than two hours to prepare himself for a face-to-face with forbidden temptation. Straightening his shoulders, he flipped the engine switch and took them back to the marina, determined to keep his mind focused on the task at hand.

Too many lives were at stake.

New York City was at stake.

His body and its prohibited needs were unimportant.

Which he reminded himself seventy minutes later as he and Silas rode in an otherwise empty elevator at DHS's NYC headquarters, ascending closer and closer toward a reunion he both dreaded and anticipated with equal fervor.

Christ, he was a SEAL, for fuck's sake. Retired or not, he'd always be a SEAL, and SEALs were not weak. *He* was in full control of his body and his actions, and he was not going to do a damn thing about his so-called attraction to one of his teammates. Hell, he hadn't seen the woman in well over a year...nearly two. He might not find her attractive now. It could've just been that forbidden shit that held the appeal.

Yeah...he nodded to himself, feeling calmer. Centered.

Now that Brian Vickers was no longer under his command, that family off-limits code technically didn't come into play—although to Archer, it would never go away. Still, it meant the attraction was no longer exactly forbidden. Perhaps that appeal had lessened too.

Bullshit.

It was stronger after reading through her file and the mission report file Silas handed him on the ride over. Despite somehow not feeling right about it, he had no choice but to read her personal file. It was normal procedure to know everything about everyone on the team he commanded and even though Sandy was exceptional, she was not an exception to that rule.

The woman had gone through a lot in her life. She was a wife and mother at age eighteen. A SEAL widow at age twenty-one. Worked as a secretary in the D.A.'s office before becoming an investigator, all while she put herself through college when Brian was school age. Obtained a BS in Homeland Security with a concentration in Intelligence. Was headhunted several times by the CIA and DHS. She chose DHS, but was currently working jointly with the CIA on this overseas chatter.

All of that information only increased her appeal.

Dammit.

"Still not a fan of elevators?" Silas asked, reminding him of their location, his buddy's gaze intent, missing nothing.

Just like the man's memory. He was no doubt referring to a joint mission over a decade ago, where Archer had been in an elevator in the basement of a building when a bomb detonated, trapping him and five others for over twelve hours. He'd been unable to save them all, and for a time, it had eaten away at him, but counseling, for the most part, had helped.

Still, if he admitted that, it would lay open for debate why he was on edge and confessing to raging hormones was not going to happen. So, he shrugged and kept things as truthful as possible. "I prefer open spaces."

Silas nodded, while a frown wrinkled his brow. "I'm guessing your boat is an exception? The living area below looked luxurious, but not exactly roomy."

"True." He smiled. "It's why I leave the doors open, so the outside is visible." Although, more often than not, he just rolled out a sleeping bag and slept on deck.

The elevator slowed to a stop and dinged for a second before the doors opened to their destination. As if in silent agreement, they ended their casual conversation, straightened their posture and strode to the reception area of that floor with their game faces on.

Most of the men and women in the building wore dress clothes. It proved his decision to take the time to stop at his place and change out of his boat-cleaning apparel before proceeding to the airport had been a good one. There was no need to impress anyone. The job was his, so he hadn't donned a monkey suit like his buddy, but he had put on a clean pair of jeans and a black button-down shirt. Good enough for a meet-n-greet and to get the job started.

Before they even got to the desk, a man with thinning hair, glasses and a ready smile came around front with his hand out. "Mr. Branson, I'm Sandy's boss, Dave Webster. Nice to meet you in person," the man said, shaking Silas' hand, then turning to him. "You must be Mr. Malone." They shook hands before the man motioned toward a hallway on the right. "Please, follow me. Sandy's waiting for you in one of the conference rooms."

He fell into step alongside Silas, more than ready to get the initial reunion out of the way so he could get down to business. But the instant he entered the conference room, he knew he was fucked.

Sandy Vickers had changed, all right. She'd become even more alluring.

Her honey blonde hair was pulled back and secured into some kind of bun that was probably meant to appear severe but only managed to look sexy. Same went for the reading glasses she pulled off her face and tossed on the table as she rose to her feet. Her white top and black skirt hugged her hourglass curves. Add that to the black heels on her feet and his body tightened favorably in response to the naughty librarian look she had going on.

Yeah, he was fucked...big time.

"...to see you in person," she was saying, shaking Silas' hand next to him.

He inhaled slowly and worked to push the fog from his brain, before she stepped in front of him and smiled. Her eyes...damn...they were even bluer than he'd remembered, and the color flooding her cheeks only deepened the shade...and his attraction to the woman.

Dammit.

"Commander Malone, so nice to see you again," she said, extending her hand. "It's been awhile."

The instant his hand closed over hers to shake it, a strange current passed through him. She must've experienced it too, because he felt her still for a beat, and her gaze widened.

"Nice to see you again, too, Ms. Vickers," he said after a quick recovery, then found himself reluctant to release her—but did—knowing it would raise brows, especially with his boss eyeing him closely.

"Please, call me Sandy," she offered.

"Then call me Archer," he respectfully countered.

She smiled up at him. "Okay, *Archer.*"

The combination of that beautiful, open smile and the sound of his name on her lips, knocked the wind out of him.

Christ...his chest felt as if he were back in that crushed elevator, struggling for air. But in a good way, if there was such a thing. Pushing it from his mind, he returned her smile and nodded, with his mouth shut. If he opened it, he was liable to do something unorthodox and stupid...like ask her out on a date.

The woman was beautiful, smart, compassionate, and now he had to add that damn current into the mix?

This job had just gotten a whole hell of a lot more difficult.

CHAPTER THREE

If there was a gene for perseverance, then Sandy Vickers was born with an oversized one. When life threw her curveballs—and it had thrown her several—she swung away at them, and swung hard. Which was exactly what she planned to do in her present predicament. The handsome, six-foot-two-inch curveball life saw fit to toss into her path would require mega-doses of perseverance for Sandy to keep her attraction to the guy from interfering with her assignment.

She'd worked too damn hard to get where she was today to screw things up by going all soft-brained and tripping over her tongue because the SEAL in charge was too gorgeous for her own good.

But it was more than his lean, muscular body, salt-n-pepper hair, mesmerizing gray eyes, and dimpled smile she found attractive. It was his can-do attitude, his quiet strength, his willingness to lend others a hand—all things she'd witnessed during visits with her Navy SEAL son when Brian had been assigned to Commander Malone's team, fresh out of BUD/S training.

Although she hadn't talked to Archer all that much during her visits, she'd been unable to stop herself from people-watching him. It was her hobby and part of her job, and she'd silently noted the way others treated him with respect and valued his opinion and...okay, the way he turned women's heads. Women of all ages, shapes, and races. She'd witnessed several of them come onto him, but he'd always gently detangle himself from their grasp or politely refuse their propositions.

The only time she'd seen distaste sour his expression was when the wife of another commander had cornered him during a family function. Compelled to help the man who helped others, Sandy found herself unable to stand by, so she'd tapped the woman on the shoulder and informed her that her husband had been looking for her. A lie, but she hadn't hesitated to spout it to get the woman to leave.

Unwilling to dissect her motivation behind that move, she'd chalked it up as her way of showing the man respect. But when she'd thought she'd seen interest momentarily flare behind those gorgeous gray eyes of his, her mind had literally blanked. No brain activity at all, just a warm, tingly numbness, and it forced her to admit she felt more than respect for the guy.

Kind of like now.

The tingly numbness was present, but her brain activity was not...except where he was concerned. Damn, he looked good in civilian clothes, too. It was the first time she'd seen him in something other than a uniform. Jeans were made for a man like Archer. That was all the attention to detail she was giving his lower half, if she wanted to hang on to some of her brain cells, which she did, although his upper half was lethal, too. His muscle definition wasn't hidden under the thin material of the black, button-down shirt stretched across his broad shoulders and chest. The way it outlined the sexy taper of his lean torso made her mouth water. His abs were flat, and she knew—she *knew*—they had to be ridged, and wondered...

She blinked and inhaled and fought past the brain fog. *Get a grip, Sandra*, she silently berated. And she was not going to think about gripping the man in front of her. No, she was not. But the strange awareness that had jolted her body to life during their handshake had been too interesting to ignore. She vowed to worry about it when she was alone later.

Now was time for work.

Luckily, Mr. Webster hadn't noticed her flustered state. He smiled at everyone and nodded toward the table. "Shall we get started?"

As Sandy retraced her steps back to her seat, she discovered distance from Archer equaled brain activity. *Thankfully*...since her brain was her livelihood, and the reason she was given this assignment.

"I know we had a video conference with you yesterday, Mr. Branson," her boss said, sitting next to her and across from Archer. "Do we need to go over things again for Mr. Malone?"

"That won't be necessary," Archer replied. "He's already brought me up to speed."

Silas took the seat on his right and stared across the table at her and Dave, and it wasn't lost on

Sandy that she faced two handsome, capable—formidable—retired SEAL commanders. "Has there been any new chatter?"

When her boss turned to her and nodded for her to answer, she glanced back at Silas and shook her head. "No. In fact, it's been a little quieter than normal."

Silas frowned. "How so?"

"We usually hear hatred about Americans and their capitalism and freedom, but today we only picked up one or two snippets."

"How many do you hear on a normal day?" Archer asked.

She spread her hands palms up. "In the double digits, at least."

Those gorgeous, gray eyes of his narrowed. "So, what does the quiet tell you?"

"Either someone is being careful not to bring attention to themselves, or it's just an off day, which does happen," she added.

Silas leaned closer to the table. "And what do you think about today's silence? What does your gut tell you?"

Pleased that the head of the DHS Secret Division—Bone Frog Command—wanted her opinion, Sandy held the man's gaze and lifted her chin. "That the silence overseas is just silence."

"Why do you think that?" he prompted.

"Because I feel the threat is already here. In the city," she stated her fears. "We need to concentrate our efforts here. It's where we'll find the chatter about the bank now. In fact, we already have."

"How so?" Silas asked again.

"We detected an uptick in the phrase 'Federal Reserve Bank' in the city's chatter this morning," she replied.

An increase like that was never good. And even though there were several Federal Reserve Banks throughout the city, only one housed the world's gold reserve. The Federal Reserve Bank *of* New York. If gold went missing, it could destabilize nations.

She noted a slight stiffening in Archer's posture, which increased the pull of material across his broad shoulders and messed with her pulse.

Her attraction to this man was going to make her coveted first joint assignment a tough one. Especially after having read his file last night.

As per protocol, her boss had given her Ret. SEAL Commander Archer Malone's file to provide insight to her new temporary boss. It'd increased her appreciation of the seasoned SEAL. For every mission noted, she knew there were others not listed. Her chest had tightened immeasurably at the thought—and at the thought of her son seeing and experiencing such horrors while slowly building a file of his own.

But it was what he'd always wanted to do and worked hard to obtain, things she could relate to and would never interfere. She'd raised Brian to be a forward thinker. To be strong, compassionate, and an advocate for the underdog. He was on his own now, and she was going to have to step back and let him live his life…and worry about him in private— every hour of every day.

Pushing thoughts of Brian aside, she refocused on what her boss was explaining to her new boss.

"We've increased the bandwidth and added more manpower," Dave was saying as they started to rise to their feet. "So, we'll alert you of the leads that need investigating."

Archer nodded. "Roger that. I'm going to head down to Liberty Street to get the lay of the land."

She gathered her laptop and reports she hadn't even needed. "Give me ten minutes to secure this and I'll be good to go."

"Wait." He frowned, pushing his chair in. "You're going out in the field?"

She nodded. "Yes."

"I thought you were my point of contact here."

Oh, boy. She smiled, despite the sinking feeling that he was not going to like what she had to say. "No. I'm hitting the streets with you."

CHAPTER FOUR

Archer swallowed back a curse while his heart rocked in his chest. "Are you a trained agent? Do you know how to shoot a gun?"

Clutching the laptop to her chest, she lifted a brow and appeared ready to reply when her boss jumped in to sing her praises.

"Oh, it's all good," Webster rushed to say. "Sandy completed special agent training and graduated top of her class." A wide smile crossed the man's face and his chest puffed out. "She did our department proud."

The woman walked around the table to where he stood with Silas, near the door. "I know how to shoot a gun. I even have a permit to carry. And before you ask, yes...I've been out in the field. So, don't worry. You don't have to be gentle with me. I'm not a virgin."

Son-of-a...

His pulse tripped, then raced at top speed. Damn...she was lethal. He heard a quiet chuckle next to him. Silas, the bastard. This wasn't funny. It wasn't Silas putting Sandy in harm's way. It was him.

How the hell had he missed all this in her file?

"It wasn't in my file." She smiled.

Christ. Was she a mind reader, too?

"Homeland likes to keep some of us off the books," she said, as if that would make him feel better.

It did not.

She divided her attention between him and Silas. "Don't worry. I'm not going to hinder the operation. I promise you, I can hold my own."

Of that, he had no doubt. What concerned him was his need to protect her. What if it interfered with the mission? This was not good.

"Besides," Webster said, cupping his shoulder, "you're a former SEAL. You'll keep Sandy safe."

His insides twisted and a weight suddenly pressed down on his shoulders. Not every mission went off without a hitch. In fact, most never went as planned. And some garnered casualties and even death, no matter how well-trained the team was, or how prepared.

"Dave, come on. What have I told you?" Sandy set her free hand on her hip and stared at her boss. "I don't need anyone to take care of me. I've been doing it my whole life."

That had been in her file.

Archer knew she'd been an only child of older parents who'd both passed before she was eighteen. She lived in foster care until then, and shortly afterward, she met Nate Vickers.

"True." Webster pushed the glasses up his nose and grinned. "But it doesn't hurt to have someone watch your back."

That was also true. And Archer would have Sandy's six. He'd never let anything happen to her, no matter what went down.

She met his gaze and patted her laptop. "I'll meet you in reception. I just have to take care of this first."

He walked with the two men, only half listening to their conversation, his mind on his job. Establishing the possibility of viable threats took top priority. And if so, then identifying the culprits, tracking them down to take them down, came next. He might pull in more than the two Knight agents from Atlantic City. Jameson also employed several more of his former SEALs down in D.C. If needed, they'd be a phone call away. It would depend on any other new developments. He was still trying to wrap his mind around the fact that Sandy wasn't going to work safely in her office behind a computer, as he'd originally thought.

And try as he might, he couldn't stop his brain from imagining the beauty brandishing a garter holster with a gun underneath that sexy, damn skirt of hers.

The weight pressing on his shoulders shifted south.

Damn. He knew instinctively, his life was never going to be the same.

"Okay," Sandy said, approaching with a laptop bag slung over her shoulder. It pulled her shirt tighter across her ample breasts, sending heat to the bulge forming behind his zipper. "I'm ready."

He wasn't. Not by a long shot. But, he was a SEAL, and great at improvising.

With the receptionist and the three visitors she was helping within earshot, along with workers passing them to get from one hall to another, he deemed the area too crowded for conversation and just nodded to her instead.

During the elevator ride to the lobby with Silas, Sandy, and two other men who'd stepped on with them, Archer shifted his stance and weighed his options. His team still had an analyst, but she was also another pair of "boots on the ground." Experience had taught him it was always beneficial to have extra.

The man in him wanted to keep her locked up and safe, but the commander in him was pleased to have an extra gun.

Halfway to the lobby, the elevator stopped, and the two men exited, leaving the three of them alone.

When the doors closed, Sandy peered around him to look at his boss. "Mr. Branson," she said, her voice sounding softer in the small confines of the elevator, and an unexpected shiver shot down his neck. "Correct me if I'm wrong, but I get the impression you have another question for me."

His friend's lips twitched. "You are correct. And astute. And please, call me Silas."

"Silas." She smiled. "What is it you want to know?"

For a split second, a devious expression appeared on Silas' face, reminding Archer of the old Crash persona from the past, but it disappeared so fast he must've imagined it. "Would you be able to take Archer back to Jersey tonight? Or should I send the chopper back for him later?"

That rat bastard son-of-a-bitch…

"I'll make sure he gets home safely," she replied, smile evident in her tone.

He glanced at Sandy to see for himself, and the sight of her biting her lip to keep from laughing canceled his annoyance and ignited something a hell of a lot more dangerous.

Hunger.

Was this how it was always going to be? Could he not look at the woman without wanting to strip her naked and lose himself inside her? *Whoa.* Where the hell had that thought come from? Damn. His attraction to Sandy was morphing at an exponential rate. And they'd only been around each other for an hour.

He watched her smile slowly disappear, and the amusement in her eyes transform into an answering heat. Red flags immediately waved wildly in his head. Her response to him hit Archer in the solar plexus with the force of an invisible right hook.

By the time the elevator reached the lobby, two things became perfectly clear.

One—he was going to kill Silas.

Two—he had no damn defense against Sandy's attraction to him.

If he dug deep, he could fight his own attraction to her…keep his thoughts and his hands to himself.

But not if she didn't want him to…

When they exited the building, he buried those thoughts—deep—and shoved on his sunglasses. Sandy was doing something on her phone, so he turned to Silas and shook hands. "Give me a day or two and I'll have a SITREP for you."

"A'ight." His buddy nodded, glancing up and down the street, before his gaze returned, and he released his hand. "Watch your six."

After they said their goodbyes, Silas got in a taxi and disappeared.

Sandy touched his arm. "This is our Uber," she said, waving her phone toward a silver sedan pulling up to the curb.

So that was what she was doing on her phone. Nodding, he eyed the driver while he stepped ahead to open the door for her then following her inside. He wasn't a fan of this system. Too easily infiltrated, but then again, the same could be said for taxis.

"I need to head home first, so I can change." She smiled apologetically.

Aware that the driver kept glancing at them in the rearview mirror, he smiled back at her. "That's fine."

It would give them a chance to talk in private to get questions out of the way and form a game plan for the day.

Besides, he was curious to see her place. If he remembered his city geography correctly, the address in her file was about six blocks over from his mother's house. And when the car pulled into a wrap-around drop-off in front of a six-story, well-maintained, brick apartment building, thirty-three minutes later, he discovered his estimation had been correct. She lived in the vicinity of his mother.

Despite the fact that a New York block was huge, and that over two million people lived in

Queens County, it was possible that the two women had crossed paths at some point.

"Thanks." Sandy tipped the driver before he had the chance.

He exited the car and held out his hand to help her from the back seat.

"Thanks," she repeated, her voice a lot softer and breathless, and his body responded to the sound with a round of goosebumps.

Silently weathering them, he nodded and forced himself to release her. "This is a nice place." He went on to tell her about his mother living nearby.

She glanced up at him, both brows raised. "Really? Wow." Then she narrowed her eyes and shook a finger at him. "Don't you dare leave the city without paying her a visit."

He chucked and used a finger to draw a cross over his heart. "Yes, ma'am."

Nodding, she smiled. "Small world...although I only moved here three years ago. Brian and I used to live in a house in the Crescent area, but once he joined the Navy and completed basic, I realized it was just too empty—too lonely—with just me, so I started looking at apartments. Brian picked this one out. He checked the security and read all the reviews. Even questioned the residents, finally deeming the place safe enough and felt better leaving me alone," she said, using a key fob to activate the sliding doors.

"I don't blame him." Shoving his sunglasses in his shirt pocket, he walked inside with her and nodded to the man behind the concierge desk who greeted Sandy by name.

Once inside the elevator, she swiped her fob and hit the button for the fourth floor then turned to face him. "I expected to be on a waiting list for a few years but got lucky. I moved in just before Brian left for BUD/S, thankfully. The last thing I wanted was him worrying about me instead of concentrating on his training and then whatever missions he completed after being assigned to your team."

He nodded again. "I tried to get my mother to move into a building like this after my dad and brother died, but she'd insisted she wanted to move to another house. It was a smaller one, though. And near her sister." He'd hated the thought of her being alone, but he'd respected her wishes.

"Sounds like it was the right decision for her." She smiled at him, and he was happy to hold her gaze and enjoy the rest of the short ride in silence…and the way color rushed up into her face, deepening the blue of her eyes.

The elevator dinged, and she blinked, and he followed her into the hall surprised to find it busy with activity. On the left, at the end, two little girls played with a dollhouse, and at the end on the right, a little boy and girl laughed as they chased each other, while an elderly lady sat on a chair in the middle of the hall, smiling at them.

"That's their grandmother," Sandy told him quietly before greeting the woman. "Hi, Mary."

"Hi, Sandy. You're home early." Holding onto the wall, the woman rose to her feet and thrust out her other hand to him. "Who do you have with you?"

33

He carefully shook the woman's boney hand. "My name's Archer. Nice to meet you, ma'am."

"Nice to meet you, too." She smiled, nodding toward Sandy, who was opening a door further down and across the hall. "You must be special, she's never brought a man home before."

An unreasonable shaft of pleasure shot through him at that knowledge. He smiled back and thanked the lady, then walked toward Sandy, sending her a warning look when she appeared about to correct the woman. Better for others to think they were a couple, rather than working together, especially given Sandy's occupation.

Unless her neighbors weren't aware of it.

Either way, it was a discussion best held in private. Feeling Mary's gaze still on them, he stopped next to Sandy and set a hand on her back. She fumbled with the doorknob a second before twisting it open.

"Got it." She smiled, and he followed her inside. "Sorry about that." She moved out of his touch and set her laptop bag on a nearby credenza. "Mary's nice, but nosey."

He'd seen too many "nice" people do bad things to give the older lady the benefit of the doubt. "Does she know what you do for a living?"

Sandy shook her head. "Other than Brian, no one knows. Everyone here thinks I work with computers." Her face was still flushed, and he was finding it hard to look away. "It's hard for you to find the good in people, isn't it?"

Taken back by her question and astuteness, he raised a brow. "Most of the time."

"Given what you've seen, it's a wonder you're not completely jaded." For several beats, her gaze bore into his, making him feel things he'd never expected, like empathy, understanding, and an acceptance...of what, he had no idea. "Make yourself at home," she said, changing the subject with a wave of her hand at her open concept living room kitchen. "I'll change into something more *touristy* and be right back."

Before he could reply, she disappeared into a room down the hall. He glanced around the spacious apartment, surprised by the size. He estimated the square footage to be more than his cottage, but the home was just as comfortable. Nothing was out of place, and yet it felt warm and inviting. His gaze lingered on the overstuffed furniture, and a gorgeous, big screen TV over a large fireplace. Archer had no trouble imagining Brian kicking back on the couch to watch a ballgame. Hell, he wouldn't mind doing that himself. He blew out a breath and his shoulders relaxed, and when his gaze fell to a row of photos on the mantle, he walked over to them.

Brian...at different ages, and some with his mom. She hadn't changed much, other than becoming more beautiful. Warmth spread across his chest, and he rubbed at it while wondering what the hell had happened to his edge?

"I'm ready," she said from behind him.

When he turned around to find her in a pair of curve-hugging jeans, a gray T-shirt with Minnie Mouse on it, and her hair pulled back in a ponytail, he found the answer to his question. *Sandy* was what happened to his edge. He literally felt his whole body soften at the sight of her.

What the hell?

"What's wrong?" She frowned and glanced down at her apparel. "Trust me, I've seen many people come to the city in clothes like these."

"It's fine," he said, forcing his stupor away. "You look good."

Shit.

That wasn't what he'd meant to say.

Her gaze softened and color made another appearance in her cheeks. "Thanks. I'll...ah, order another Uber."

"Make sure you submit receipts. The government can pay for it, not you," he said. "And we need to talk before we proceed any further."

"Okay." She sat down on the armrest of the couch and held his gaze.

"All I want to do is establish a baseline today," he said, leaning his back against the mantle. "As well as see if anything feels off."

She nodded. "And we don't want to draw attention to ourselves, hence my tourist costume."

He smiled. The woman could wear a paper bag, and men would notice her.

"Even though it's the financial district, most of the people on the streets are from out of state, making their way to or from the 9/11 Memorial," she said, unaware that her words momentarily severed the oxygen supply to his body. "We need to blend in, so no one notices us."

Drawing in several slow, deep breaths, he nodded, feeling more in control. "We're on the same page, then. And you won't be shocked if I grab your hand or slip my arm around you if the situation calls for it."

Fishing a purse from her laptop bag, she stilled a second before nodding. "No...that'll be fine," she said, slipping the long strap across her body, and it settled snuggly between her breasts, making him envious as hell of a piece of leather. "What about a gun?"

Gun?

He blinked, and the heat in his body ran cold. "What about it?"

"Are you carrying?" she asked. "And do you want me to take mine?"

He'd considered leaving his SIG in the safe in his bedroom. Today was preliminary shit, so it shouldn't be needed. Although, there'd been plenty of times that theory had been proven wrong. Hence the reason it was strapped to his ankle. "Leave yours here. We're not infiltrating anything or sticking our noses where they don't belong. Yet."

She grabbed half of her ponytail in each hand and tugged. He wasn't sure what she'd tried to accomplish, but apparently, she succeeded because she lowered her hands and turned to him. "Got ya. We need our eyes today, not our guns. But if we do, I'm taking your evasion of my inquiry to mean you're carrying."

His lips twitched. "Something like that."

Forty minutes later, adrenaline rushed through his body as they strolled hand-in-hand down Liberty Street. It felt great to finally do a little recon. And, admittedly, it felt even better to hold Sandy's hand.

Archer's mind was boggled at how something so simple, so trivial, could have such a huge impact on his pulse. The damn thing hadn't leveled off since they'd entwined their fingers ten minutes ago.

And the air…*Christ*, it felt heavy, tangible—charged—around them. Only trouble was he didn't know if their chemistry was the cause or if something was off.

Or both.

"Oh, babe, look." She tugged him to a hot dog vendor set up right across the street from the bank entrance. "What do you think?"

He grinned. Perfect. "Let's eat." It'd give him a chance to survey the area while they took their time enjoying their food. The last time he had a street vendor hot dog was over a decade ago.

"What would you like?" Average height, average build, the twenty-something Hispanic man split his gaze between them.

"Hi…ah…" Sandy stepped closer to the guy and smiled, waiting for him to supply his name.

The man smiled back. "Rodrigo."

"I'd like a hot dog with mustard, please, Rodrigo," she replied, and glanced at him. "What about you, babe?"

"Two with ketchup," he said, ordering his heating body to cool it. She only used the endearment as a cover.

"Have you ever run out of hot dogs, Rodrigo?" she asked, chatting up the vendor while he filled her order, allowing Archer to study the bank behind his sunglasses.

No one went in or out. The whole façade was unobtrusive. And most of the foot traffic occurred on their side of the street.

"Mmm…" Sandy moaned, slowly chewing her first bite, and stopping his damn heart.

Every part of his body stilled, then some of his favorite parts twitched. Even Rodrigo stilled, and his face was red as he fumbled with Archer's order.

Poor guy. The woman was lethal and had no clue.

He paid for their food, and they walked a few feet away to allow the man to wait on three others who stopped. Sandy stood facing him, and together they ate while they each scanned the area in front of them.

"I have an idea," she said, digging out her phone. "I know we have access to the street cameras, but I don't think it'll hurt to grab a few still shots."

He nodded. "Agreed."

She immediately moved closer to take a selfie of them, capturing more of the building and the people behind them rather than their faces. "Oh, wait," she said in an excited, loud tone. "I should get one of Rodrigo and me." She rushed to the vendor who stood alone by his cart again. "If that's okay?"

"Sure." A wide grin split the guy's face as Sandy snapped away.

Archer moved forward. "Here, let me." He took the phone from her and stepped back, getting a much wider scope on the shot. "Perfect."

"Thanks, babe," she said, then turned to Rodrigo. "And thank you for the hot dog. It was delicious."

He grinned. "My pleasure. Enjoy your visit to the city."

Archer moved close and slid his arm around her waist. "We will. Thanks." After they walked a half a block, he stopped and turned to her. "I think you're on to something with these photos."

For the next hour and a half, they canvased the bank and surrounding blocks in a zigzagging, chaotic pattern, using both of their phones to take selfies, photos with other vendors, and some with the city's more colorful characters. They even snapped a few with other tourists, all to make it look legit. Thanks to Sandy's brilliant idea and the way she worked the crowd, he got a good bead on the location and already had some ideas to discuss with the team when he got together with them back in Jersey tomorrow.

Right now, though, he was more concerned about the bald bruiser with a tattoo of an eye on the back of his head. Three times they'd changed blocks, and the man always showed up. Could be coincidence. Could be he planned to rob them. Could be the guy was someone of interest and he was suspicious of them.

Could be nothing.

Whatever the reason, it was time to get a reaction.

Archer slowed them to a stop near a quiet corner and leaned his head to the right to whisper in her ear, "Don't be alarmed, but I want to check something out."

"The left-handed, bald man with the eye tattoo, and missing right pinky?" She stepped in front of him to play with his collar. "Me, too."

Shit.

He set his hands on her waist and twisted them around so he could lean his back against the building and keep an eye on the guy. "You noticed, too?"

Christ. She'd noticed a lot more than he had about their tail.

"That's why I get paid the big bucks." She chuckled. "And I'm positive we have several photos of him, so I'm going to start with him."

"Good," he said, eyeing the guy pretending to look at postcards outside a souvenir store across the street. "It's time we push him for a reaction." He cupped her face. "Okay?"

He felt her breath hitch. "Okay," she whispered, and when her gaze dropped to his mouth, his breathing wasn't all that steady, either.

CHAPTER FIVE

Since the two of them had been masquerading as a couple and needed to maintain the façade, Archer knew he had to just jump right in, which sucked. He wanted to savor the first brush of their lips and the taste of her, but he had to make it look like they knew each other's bodies, and their wants and needs.

He was relying on their chemistry to help him out.

Her hand slid up his chest, over his shoulders, and when her thumbs brushed his neck, heat rushed through his body. This time, he didn't ignore the hunger she induced. He embraced it, dragging her against him as he covered her mouth with his, taking the kiss he'd thought about for the past three years.

Over and over, he plundered, discovering her taste, her essence, loving the way she melted into him while her tongue brushed his on a demanding mission of her own.

His body was rock-hard, and temperature was already at inferno, so when she pressed against him, practically climbing up his body, he shook with the need to be inside her.

They went from zero to one-hundred-and-ten-percent inside of sixty seconds.

It was insane and amazing, and he knew it. He *knew* kissing this woman would be the closest thing to heaven he'd ever experience on this earth.

Finally touching her, tasting her, it was unforgettable...like their mission.

Shit. He stiffened and forced his mouth to release hers.

"Well...?" Resting her forehead on his chin, she panted, her hot breaths teasing his throat. "What...did he...do?"

Archer blinked the world back into focus and noted the empty corner across the street. "He left."

She drew back to frown up at him, but still held on to his shoulders. "You sure?"

He swept his gaze up and down the block and nodded. "Yeah, he's headed south on Greenwich." That damn tattoo glared at him, as if keeping an eye on them.

"What do you think that means?"

Amid protests from his body, Archer released her, and when she stepped back, he straightened from the wall. "We either put his fears to rest, or bought some time."

Her gaze snapped to his, and she frowned. "Time for what?"

Blowing out a breath, he shook his head. "I don't know."

But he intended to find out.

***

Sandy was in trouble. Dimpled, gray-eyed, broad-shouldered, testosterone-filled trouble. Kissing the guy yesterday when they'd been pretending to be a couple had been necessary, but in a way...earth-shattering.

At the first brush of his lips, every erogenous zone in her body woke up. And not just the neglected ones. No. Some she didn't even know existed. They shouted to the heavens, demanding more. She always knew her reaction to him would be intense. It was a given. A fact. Her body had alluded to it ever since her son had introduced them the first time she'd visited Brian on base in Virginia.

But what really shocked her, had been Archer's reaction to her. It was as if he couldn't get enough. He devoured her, kissed her like she was the best thing he'd ever tasted.

God...that'd been empowering. And had knocked every single thought from her mind.

How was that possible?

Wrong question. Why did it matter?

It didn't. She had a *job* to do. Not a SEAL.

At that thought, heat shot through her belly and funneled to places further south.

Not good.

"Oh...I know that look," her friend and co-worker, Barbara Harmon said, walking into the office they shared, the morning sun pouring in through their floor-to-ceiling window, glinting off the golden highlights in her red hair. "You were thoroughly and feverishly kissed."

As much as she wanted to deny it to herself, there was no way Sandy could fool her analyst friend. Like her, the woman made a living out of spotting things others didn't see.

Sandy blew out a breath and sat back in her chair. "Yeah. And it's not good."

A smile twitched Barbara's lips as she sat on the corner of Sandy's desk and folded her arms across her chest, looking like a woman who just turned thirty-five, not forty-five. "Looks to me like it was very good. And that's the problem."

She snorted. "Bingo."

"Why would it be a bad thing, though?" Her friend frowned. "You haven't had sex in over two years. Before that it was five. And before that, you were married. Your ability to abstain is astounding."

Since this was a discussion they'd held countless times, Sandy remained quiet. There wasn't anything she could add that she hadn't said over the past decade.

"You can't use your son as an excuse to run blocker." Barbara shook her head, and the sun haloed her highlights again. "He's living his own life, and it's time you lived yours."

She sighed. "You don't understand."

Barbara snickered. "I do. Only too well…and…Oh. My. God…" Her friend jumped off the desk and slapped a hand to her chest. "It was that hunk of a SEAL in black you left with yesterday. The one in charge of the special job you're working on. Brian's former commander?"

Sandy dropped her head into her hands and mumbled, "Yes," through her fingers.

Dropping down into her own chair, Barbara whistled. "Wow. You were right. You always told me the guy was super-hot."

She mumbled something unintelligible, because it was all her thoughts could offer up.

"But...I don't see the issue, Sandy." Barbara stared at her with concern in her light blue eyes. "You kissed the guy. You liked it. Did he not like it?"

A snort shot up her throat. "Let's just say, we both liked it. But that's the problem, Barb. We're working together on a case that has a lot of people's lives at stake. I can't forget my obligations to them because he makes me feel good."

"Ohhh..." Barb bit her lip and squinched her nose. "He makes you feel good? Do you hear yourself? You've never said that about anyone before." She leaned forward and slapped the edge of Sandy's desk. "You *have* to let happen whatever is going to happen. You just have to, Sandy. You deserve it."

"Not at the expense of my brain cells, because that's the first thing to disappear when he's near," she said with a shake of her head, before sipping her now cold cup of coffee.

"You should have sex with him."

Even though the coffee had thankfully cleared her throat, she choked anyway. "Barb," she ground out, getting up to shut their door a little too late. "Watch what you say. I don't need Dave to half-hear our conversation and pull me from this case."

A contrite look crossed her friend's face. "Sorry, I should've shut the door, but I still stand by my suggestion. If you have sex with the guy, then maybe it'll get rid of the intense craving and allow your brain cells to coexist with him in a room."

Sandy couldn't help but chuckle at the absurdity of her friend's suggestion and admit that it actually held merit. "But what if once isn't enough?"

"Then jump his bones morning, noon, and night." Barbara grinned. "He looked very sturdy to me. He could handle it."

She exhaled and shook her head. "I think it would kill me."

"Yeah, but what a way to go..." Barb held her gaze and grinned. "Death by *SEAL* injection."

Oh, my God. Sandy snorted, then slapped a hand over mouth to keep from laughing too loudly.

It didn't work.

The woman was a piece of work, and a good friend. And Sandy would've told her that, if Dave hadn't knocked on the door and peeked his head inside.

"Mr. Malone wants to video conference," he told her.

Already?

After uploading the photos from both of their phones to her laptop last night, she'd asked if he wanted her to head with him to New Jersey or to stay in the city and go through the photos. Thankfully, he'd opted for the latter. Being cooped up with Archer in the close quarters of a vehicle after he'd kissed her senseless would've asked for trouble.

Silently breathing a sigh of relief, she'd insisted he drove her SUV home—after he visited his mother. He thanked her, promising to bring it back in a day or two, agreed to stop in and see his mom before leaving Queens, then headed for the basement garage where she'd told him he'd find her vehicle.

It sat there most weeks, unless she headed to Virginia Beach to visit Brian. She never drove in the city, so she wouldn't need it.

"He's already on a secure line in Op Room 2," her boss informed.

Ignoring Barbara's teasing smile, Sandy grabbed her notes and some of the photos she'd printed out last night, and followed Dave past two agents talking to Amy at reception and down the opposite hall to the meeting, surprised when he didn't stay and closed the door behind her instead.

"Good morning, Sandy," Archer greeted, and her body didn't seem to care that he was on a screen and not actually there in person.

It heated in response, anyway. "Good morning," she replied, unsure whether to sit or stand, so she set her stuff on the table before turning to face the screen.

Larger than life, he appeared to be sitting at a desk, talking to her through a webcam in his laptop. His hair was damp, as if freshly showered. Little droplets of water dripped onto his shoulder, the moisture deepening the gray of his T-shirt. He had a sexy, five o'clock shadow scruff on his strong jaw even though it was barely half past eight in the morning.

"So…what's up?" She rested her butt on the edge of the table and cocked her head.

Reaching for a coffee mug on his desk, he arched a brow. "You tell me. I got your text to call in and conference."

Sandy heart rolled as it dropped into her stomach. "Archer," she said, straightening from the table. "I never sent you a text."

He stiffened. "Get out of the room, Sandy. Now!" he barked.

Heart in her throat, she raced for the door, twisted the handle but it wouldn't budge. She turned to face Archer. "I can't. It's locked."

CHAPTER SIX

Sandy heard Archer mumble something about Dave under his breath.

"His damn phone is going straight to voicemail," he growled at the phone in his hand.

There had to be an explanation. She refused to believe her boss had anything to do with whatever was going on. She shook the door and pounded on it, but knew it was no use. Unless someone happened to be walking by, no one would hear her. The secure conference rooms were at the end of the hall for privacy. Access was granted through a keypad and the security code changed twice a day. There were no windows, and only the one door to go in or out.

"Do you have your phone?" Archer asked, grabbing his off a table and punching in a few numbers.

She shook her head. "They're not allowed in here per protocol."

He muttered an oath, and appeared to be punching numbers in to his phone again. "Come on, come on. Pick up," he growled, holding it to his ear.

She eyed the console on the wall.

"No, Sandy," Archer said. "Don't touch the equipment. It might drop our call. I'm calling building security now. You keep trying the door."

She rattled the handle a few times and pounded on the door again, but nothing happened. Then she heard a hiss in the corner by the trash can, and a pungent smell filled the air a second before a flash of fire appeared and flames shot out of the can.

Dammit. Her pulse pounded in her ears, as she glanced up at the ceiling, willing the sprinkler system to kick in.

It didn't.

If an accelerant was used, she didn't think water would have much effect anyway. Trying to turn the can over to snuff it out was out of the question, because the flames were already melting the can.

"...in a video conference room on the fourteenth floor." Archer paced as he spoke into his phone. "I don't care what your instruments say. There's a fucking fire. I'm watching it now. Sandy Vickers is stuck in there. She can't. The door is locked. Stop arguing with me and get upstairs and help her, goddammit."

Sandy had learned a long time ago not to wait around for help. She'd survived on her own. No one was going to help her now, either. Archer was doing all that he could, but he was too far away.

Eyeing the door, she chewed her lip. Popping the pins on the hinges wouldn't work. Access was triggered by—

"The keypad," Archer said. "Good girl. Estimate it on the other side, measure two palms down and bust the wall, Sandy."

With no hammer or anything like it available in the room, she knew it was either going to be her fist, elbow, knee, or foot. If the wall was steel reinforced, then her fist wasn't a good option. Hell, none of them were. Self-defense classes had taught her that an elbow or knee had more impact than a fist, and two decades of tai chi had strengthened both.

But before she could make up her mind, the power went out, taking the lights and her connection to Archer with it. The flames provided light, so with one hand holding her shirt over her nose and mouth, she used the other to steady herself and began to kick at the wall. Over and over she slammed her foot into the solid surface, glad she wore her sturdy black heels because they punctured the sheetrock.

Letting go of her shirt, she dropped to her knees, grabbed the busted drywall and ripped pieces of it away. The air was hot and suffocating, and she could feel the flames getting closer. She had to get out...now. Holding her breath, she reached inside the hole, felt around until her fingers came in contact with wires then she yanked them hard. They broke free, and a second later, she heard the door click.

Sandra scrambled to her feet and tugged on the handle, relief shooting through her when it opened. She stumbled into the hallway as security raced toward her.

Then the fire alarms started to blare.

Several men rushed into the burning conference room with fire extinguishers, while three others helped her to a chair in the reception area and shoved an oxygen mask on her. "Stay calm. The paramedics and fire department are on their way."

She hoped they put the fire out before it spread any further. Dave and Barbara exited a research room, and she watched them hurry down the hall toward the stairs with other workers, until Barb spotted her.

"Oh my God, Sandra...are you okay?" Her friend rushed to her side.

"What happened?" Dave asked, glancing from her to the commotion down the hall, his face paling. "Is there an actual fire?"

She nodded. "Phone," she croaked out, and removed the mask so they'd hear. "Call Archer."

The poor guy had to be going nuts. She knew she would've if the shoe had been on the other foot.

"Keep that on, miss," the security guy lectured, battling with her to put the mask back in place.

"Archer," she uttered again.

Barb nodded and touched Dave's arm. "She wants you to call Archer to let him know she's okay."

"Oh. Yeah. Okay." He dug his phone from his pocket and dialed. "Mr. Malone? It's Dave. Sandy wanted me to call to tell you she's okay." He pulled the phone away from his ear and frowned at it. Then put it back and met her gaze. "I-I don't understand. I wasn't in there because you texted me beforehand and told me the conference was between you and Sandy. You didn't need me in there."

More relief ripple through her. She knew there had to be an explanation. Then a shaft of anger

53

pierced her chest. It still had to be someone from DHS to have access to that room. They had to have knowledge of equipment, too. Who the hell was manipulating them? She glanced around at the faces in front of her, knowing—with the exception of Barb and Dave—it could possibly be one of them. All she saw were concerned expressions.

"Get these people out of here." Another security guard came over and motioned toward the stairs. "Let's go. Move her outside. The paramedics are waiting."

The next ten minutes were a blur as she was helped down fourteen flights of stairs to the sidewalk outside where she was met by a team of paramedics, who ushered her to the back of an open ambulance.

As they checked her over and she answered their questions, as well as those from several firefighters who asked her about the firebomb, her mind started to work on the puzzle of who could've orchestrated today's events...and why?

And why was she so tired all of a sudden? And hallucinating? Had to be because a very familiar, broad, former Navy SEAL appeared out of the crowd and strode straight for her, determination, anger, and concern tightening his jaw.

Only he wasn't a hallucination. He was real. And warm. She knew this, because when she removed her oxygen mask, pushed off the back of the ambulance and stood—albeit haphazardly, with only one shoe—she was suddenly crushed against his wonderful...*tangible*...hard chest.

"Sandy," he muttered near her ear, his warm breath heating her neck. "Thank God."

Archer...

Slipping her arms around his back, she relaxed against him and held on tight. "I'm okay," she mumbled, shaking.

Or was that him?

Didn't matter. Neither did remaining strong. Not with him. Sandy knew—with Archer—she could drop her armor for just a minute, let go of her control and allow someone else to be strong for her. Settling against him, she relished the feel of his strong arms banded around her, and the feel of his heart beating strong and sure...and damn, she needed this...hadn't realized just how much she needed him to just hold her while she soaked up his warmth and strength.

But only for a minute.

Feeling better, she drew back, although not all the way out of his embrace, to stare into his face. "How'd you get here so fast? Has it been three hours?"

She had no idea how much time had passed since that video screen had gone dark, but he was here now, in the flesh, all the way from the Jersey shore.

Still holding her with one arm, he used his free hand to gently stroke her cheek. "It's been an hour. I took a chopper. Two of our other team members are on their way, one is driving your SUV."

She nodded, curious to meet the others. She thought she'd heard one of them was another woman.

He dipped down to peer straight into her eyes. "You sure you're okay?"

"Yeah." She nodded again. "Although I broke two nails. And a shoe."

Chuckling, he kissed her forehead and banded his arms around her again. It was a little slice of heaven in her hellish morning, so she enjoyed it for a beat, smiling when she caught sight of Barb, still hovering nearby, giving her two thumbs up.

"Can she go?" Archer asked the paramedics behind her.

"Yes," she answered for herself, having already refused transport to the hospital.

He glanced from her back to the paramedics and lifted a brow, apparently not willing to take her word for it.

"Yes," someone said behind her. "Just keep an eye on her. If she's nauseated, coughing, dizzy, has chest pains, or blurry vision, call 911 immediately."

"Roger that," Archer replied, his serious gaze boring into hers, as if waiting for her to acknowledge.

She nodded and his gaze softened.

"Let's get you out of here," he said, slipping an arm around her shoulders.

She began to walk choppily because her other shoe was no doubt stuck in a piece of wall in that conference room. A frown pulled at her brow. She loved those shoes, dammit. An innocent casualty, along with everything else she'd left in there.

Sandy stiffened and halted. "Wait. I can't leave without my laptop and purse." If either went missing, she had irreplaceable things inside them both. Some pertaining to this case…some personal. Either way… "I'm not leaving without them."

"Forget it," he practically growled. "No way are you going back in that building."

She pulled him aside and leaned in close. "Look, I'm sure the fire consumed my notes and the photos I brought to the meeting, but I have them all saved on my computer. They, or something else we captured yesterday, must be the reason behind this incident. I'll be damned if someone gets them, too."

His gaze narrowed a second before he nodded. "I'll take care of it," he said, then turned and disappeared into the crowd before she could ask how, since the fire department had the building on lockdown.

Ten minutes later, Archer emerged through the crowd with her purple laptop bag in hand, the decidedly feminine floral print in no way diminishing his masculinity.

Once again, he strode right to her, oblivious to the numerous female heads he turned, and an unguarded thrill shot down to her toes. "Here you go. I shoved your purse inside the bag, too."

"Thank you." She smiled at him while taking the laptop bag from him. "How did you get inside?"

Barb shook her head. "Don't ask him that. If he tells you, he'll have to kill you."

Amusement flickered through her as she shook her head at her friend. "Think that applies to assassins, Barb." Although, he'd no doubt filled that roll a few times during his SEAL days. She turned her attention back to him. "Seriously, though, Archer. Thank you so much. How did you get these from my desk? It was locked." The keys had been in her purse.

"I know," he replied, a slight twitch to his lips. "You may need a new desk. And a new door."

She snickered. Damn...she really liked this guy.

A second later, he produced her missing shoe as if out of thin air, and her heart caught on the unexpected, thoughtful, sweet gesture.

"How...?" she started to ask, then shut her mouth when he squatted down to slip it on her bare foot.

His touch was gentle and warm and deliciously calloused, and liquid heat shot straight up her body mingling with a host of emotions the damn man was awakening in her.

"Is everything okay now?" he asked, rising to stand in front of her, his gaze serious again. "Are we good to go?"

Swallowing past a heated, swollen throat, she nodded and slung the strap of her laptop bag over her shoulder. Everything was *so* okay it was bad, and they were better than good, which was the problem.

He slid an arm around her waist, nodded to Barb, then guided her to where Dave stood talking to his boss and several policemen and firemen. "You and I will be chatting at a later date," he told her boss before walking with her toward a taxi waiting at the curb. "Before we go any further, we need to remove the batteries from our phones."

Good idea. Sandy dug her purse out of her laptop bag, then her cell from her purse and removed her battery. Her chest tightened at the thought of someone getting information off her phone. She didn't care about her, but her son's number and their texts were on it. She shoved the two pieces back in her purse and shook. "So help me, Archer, if someone uses any of this to get to Brian I'll—"

"Hey…" He turned her to face him. "It's just a precaution. We don't know if they're compromised. There are several ways I could've received that false text from you this morning."

"And Dave from you," she added.

He blinked. Twice. "Possibly. I have an expert standing by to examine our phones. And if tampering is determined, we'll handle it. I promise."

She clenched her jaw and nodded, feeling slightly less stressed.

No one better threaten her son. No one.

"Okay, *momma bear*. Let's get you out of here," he said, dimple appearing as he held the taxi door open for her, waiting until she got settled before sliding in next to her.

As soon as he shut the door, the taxi pulled away, leading Sandy to conclude Archer had ordered this ride earlier. It's the reason it was already at the curb *and* why the driver hadn't waited for them to give him her address. It'd already been given.

At least…she had assumed Archer was taking her home, but when the cab crossed the Williamsburg Bridge and headed south, she turned to the SEAL in charge next to her and frowned. "Where are we going?"

He leaned close and spoke low, "Somewhere safe," his gaze a mixture of contradictions—with concern and stubbornness vying for top position.

"But—"

He silenced her with a finger pressed softly to her lips. "It's not up for debate."

CHAPTER SEVEN

Not up for debate?

Sandra raised a brow.

It would be…when they were alone.

She must look like she'd gone ten rounds with a fireplace…and lost. Dust or ash streaked her clothes, which smelled like smoke. She'd lay odds her face was streaked with the stuff too. And her bun felt lopsided. She needed a shower and change of clothes—and a drink…even if it was still technically morning.

Right now, though, he could have this win. They weren't alone, so she wasn't going to argue about where they were going.

She nodded, and the movement caused her mouth to brush his finger. Heat flashed in his eyes, deepening the gorgeous gray color to a delicious slate hue. His jaw worked a time or two before he removed his touch and straightened in his seat. She glanced out her window and watched the Brooklyn streets go by and absently wondered if she was sitting next to Captain America.

A smile tugged her lips. She supposed Archer could be considered a more mature version of Chris Evans. Eying the stoic man sitting next to her, she didn't know what was driving her crazier, the silence, or the chemistry zinging between them.

Both were a problem. One was fixable. The silence was, because he didn't want to be overheard. It made sense. She agreed. The other, though? The chemistry? That was the elephant in the...cab.

According to the clock on the dash, they'd been in the taxi twenty-eight minutes. So, after enduring nearly that length of charged silence, Sandy was happy when the cab finally stopped at a local pizzeria. One of her favorites, actually.

Augustine's was a gem of a discovery from way back when she used to bring Brian down to play ball during the summers. The two of them had been coming back ever since. Now...it was just her, although, not as often.

While Archer paid for the cab, she pushed her nostalgia aside, and got out. Exiting on his side hadn't been an option. That would've ensured physical contact with the guy, and she was still a little too unstable to tempt fate. Ignoring his frown, she walked around the cab to the sidewalk, doing her best to brush off her clothes, tighten her bun, and hopefully, wipe off whatever soot was on her face.

As for the smoky smell of her clothes? She was out of luck.

God, she was tired. The aroma of marinara wafted around them, and her stomach promptly growled.

Tired *and* hungry.

Archer stepped close. "You missed a spot," he said, lifting a hand to brush her jaw with his thumb.

So much for avoiding physical contact. Awareness shot down to her toes and bounced back up.

That was new.

She cleared her throat. "Thanks...So...since the cab is gone, and we no longer have wheels, I'm guessing that 'someplace safe' you mentioned is close?"

"Almost," he said.

"So why are we here?"

His dimples appeared. "For pizza." He must've sensed her impatience, because he reached for her hand and squeezed. "Just hang in there a little longer. I promise we'll talk."

When she nodded, he led them inside, and she noted the place was empty except for two elderly patrons sharing a corner table while enjoying a heated discussion about spring training.

Archer led her to the counter where he released her hand to...pay for a pizza?

When had he ordered that?

His phone was battery-less like hers. She'd assumed they were coming inside to order a pie, not pick one up.

"Archer, you old, frogman! I thought that was you! Come on back." The elderly owner waved from the kitchen through the small pass-through window.

He grabbed the pizza with one hand and her hand with his other and headed through a swinging door into the kitchen. It was vacant, except for the owner. "Hi, Gus." Archer smiled, shaking the old man's hand. "How've you been?"

Her mind reeled. He knew Gus, too?

The owner's gaze fell on her, and he grinned. "Not as good as you if you're here with Sandy." He pushed Archer aside to pull her in for their ritual hug. The octogenarian always remembered her, no matter how many months passed between her visits.

"You're too sweet." Smiling, she hugged him quickly, hoping he didn't notice her *eau de smoke* scent.

"Nonsense." He shook his head and stepped back. "I'm honest. You're a doll, and I can see he agrees with me, too." Gus set a hand on Archer's shoulder before meeting her gaze. "And you could never find a better man than a Malone. I served with his father. Was best man at his parent's wedding. Was his brother's godfather. Wept like a baby the day his father and brother died. Still do, every September."

Archer stiffened next to her. She automatically reached out to set a hand on his back.

"I was there the day this frogman enlisted," Gus continued, face beaming. "He's a hero, Sandy. You hold on to him. In fact, you both hold onto each other. It does this old heart good to see two wonderful people finding each other."

Gus' gaze grew misty, and she felt a pang of guilt at letting him believe they were a couple, especially since he had such wonderful history with Archer's family. But not knowing if it was important to maintain the ruse they started yesterday, she remained quiet.

"It was great seeing you again, Gus," Archer said.

Releasing his shoulder, the old man nodded. "You, too, Archer," he said, and dug a set of car keys from his pocket.

Wait a minute...

Her car keys.

How?

Gus dropped them into Archer's outstretched hand and waved at the back door. "It's parked out there."

Nodding, Archer led her outside, where they found her SUV parked behind the dumpster.

"How?" she asked out loud that time.

He smiled, unlocked the doors and held hers opened while she got in. "I'll explain in a minute."

Nodding, she took the pizza from him and waited while he shut her door, walked around to the driver's side and climbed in. "Your minute's up."

He started the engine and chuckled. "Your minutes are quick."

As much as she liked how amusement relaxed his expression, she had too many questions and needed answers. "How did my car get here? Didn't you say you said you took a chopper to the city this morning?"

"I did," he replied, glancing at her. "I also contacted Gus before I left Jersey to ask if a friend could drop this vehicle off behind his pizzeria so I could pick it up."

Okay... "But why here?"

He shifted her SUV into reverse and backed out onto the street. "Because, even though we swept this for bugs, I didn't want to risk someone spotting it in the city if you're on someone's radar." He shoved it into drive and headed southwest, zigzagging through several streets. "Plus, the safe house we're using is close by."

In less than five minutes, he pulled into the parking lot of a vacant warehouse and drove around the dilapidated building toward the old docks out back.

"Good choice. I feel safe already," she said, half amused, half weary as he maneuvered through a large opening in a busted bay door. "If there's no running water in here, I can always jump into the East River out back, to wash this smoke off me."

"There's plenty hot water inside. Trust me," he said, smirk dimpling his cheek.

There was just enough arrogance in the tilt of his chin to give her pause for thought. He was up to something. Just like at the pizza shop, there was more than meets eye here. She remained quiet and watchful, and a little bit excited to see exactly what he had up his sleeve…besides solid muscles.

He drove through a large room with a high, steel-beamed ceiling surrounded by busted windows and around an old, rusted conveyer belt, then through an oversized door, into an area with no windows and only one door. He parked in front of it.

"Okay, this room doesn't look like it's about to fall apart," she said. "So, I'm guessing there's livable space behind that steel door?"

"Something like that." He took the pizza from her. "Come on. I know you're tired."

She nodded. "My head is spinning, but it's because I'd like to know what's going on."

After unlocking the door, he stepped aside for her to enter, and she was surprised to find herself in a lit stairwell that only headed in one direction—down. Descending the four flights, she noted the walls were solid concrete with no windows. At the bottom, Archer unlocked the lone door, using a combination of keystrokes on a keypad to the right, similar to the one outside the conference room that morning.

What if they got locked inside? Her chest unexpectedly tightened. Busting this wall was not an option. It, too, was solid concrete. A shudder ran unchecked down her body.

And wouldn't stop.

Dammit.

Archer opened the door then took one look at her and frowned. "Hey. It's okay," he said, ushering her inside a large, open-concept apartment.

The ceilings were vaulted, and the space felt anything but closed in. She breathed a little easier. There were couches and tables and chairs, a big screen TV, a workout space in the far-right corner, a hallway to the right, and a set of stairs at the far-left that led to another hallway. The place was huge.

He set the pizza down on a kitchen island, before turning to face her. "You're okay. Here, let me take that." He removed the laptop bag from her shoulder and placed it next to the pizza.

"I know," she said, still shaking. She wrapped her arms around herself and blew out a breath. "Sorry. I don't know what's wrong with me."

Holding her gaze, he ran his hands up and down her arms. "Shock is setting in. You've been through a lot today."

She lifted a shoulder, and by concentrating on the feel of his hands brushing her skin, some of her disquiet settled. Just like in front of headquarters earlier, his delicious warmth seeped through her, and until that moment, Sandy hadn't realized how cold she felt inside.

"Hey, come here. I got you," he murmured, pulling her into him, and she sighed when his arms banded around her again.

All the questions she had would have to wait. Right now, she just needed *this*. Needed to soak up this man's strength and warmth again. To give her mind and body a chance to rest and reset.

She slid her arms around the man and burrowed in, and judging by the tight hold he had on her, she got the impression he needed this, too. Unsure of how long it took, eventually her shaking stopped…and the embrace changed. Awareness crackled around them and a different type of heat invaded her body.

"Better?" he asked, his voice deliciously low near her ear.

Every part of her was aware of every part of him, and although she knew she should draw back and thank him for being kind, her body refused to listen to her mind. Need was taking over, recalling yesterday's kiss. What had started out as a ruse had instantly morphed into a hot, teasing, tasting, tangle of desire she hadn't expected. Now that desire was back, hoping for another round. But that was so unwise.

She inhaled and nodded. "Yeah, I just...thanks."

Damn, he made thinking difficult.

Sandy focused on the living room visible behind him, noting the open area felt smaller and a hell of a lot more intimate than when they'd walked in. After several silent seconds ticked by and he didn't make any move to release her, she shifted back enough to glance at his face. "Something wrong?"

He shook his head and remained silent, but the heat in his eyes spoke loud and clear. He was remembering that kiss...and wanted another, too. Her body trembled against his very hot, very hard body, needing what he wanted to give.

With the sexiest sound rumbling in his throat, Archer's hand glided up her spine to cup the back of her head while his mouth crashed over hers, kissing her long and deep and frantic.

He devoured her strength and demolished her brain cells, drinking, taking, seeking, as if he needed to reassure himself that she was okay. Damn, he was a force of nature. And so hungry. So was she.

Sandy met his tongue stroke for stroke, and when he lifted her up and set her on the counter, she was grateful she wore a loose skirt when he moved to stand between her thighs. He had her pulse pounding and body shaking, reminding her that she was alive. She wrapped her legs around him and pulled him closer.

A deep, sexy groan rumbled in his chest, and he rocked against her. Sandy moaned, heat pooling low in her belly. She returned the favor, rubbing against the large bulge in his jeans, nearly coming undone.

He broke the kiss to suck in air. "Damn, Sandy," he muttered against her neck. "I have zero control with you." Then he was kissing her throat while his hands skimmed down her sides.

"Me too." She dropped her hands to his lean hips, her mind and body unable to process all the sensations rushing through her.

The sound of a heavy door closing in the outside stairwell echoed with a muffled thud. They broke apart, and Archer helped her down before moving several feet away to the sink. Working to catch her breath, she watched the muscles ripple across his back and shoulders as he gripped the counter.

Damn, that was close. Last thing she wanted was to meet the other team members with her tongue down the boss's throat.

He turned around and met her gaze. "You good?"

She snorted. Nowhere near it. "As I can be, today."

His gaze softened, but he remained by the sink. "A shower, some pizza, and shop-talk should help."

Sandy nodded, knowing full well it wasn't food she was hungry for, but was hopeful the arrival of others would cool the chemistry between them.

***

Recovering his wits enough to walk around to the other side of the island and open the pizza box, Archer had just taken a bite of a slice when the rest of the team walked in with bags in their hands.

"Supply run," the long haired, red-headed computer expert, TJ Lynch, stated unnecessarily. His eyes lit up. "Oh, pizza." He dropped his bags by the wall, rushed over to grab a slice and thrust his free hand to Sandy. "I'm TJ. Handsome hacker, wisecracker extraordinaire at your service, ma'am."

Sandy laughed, and the lighthearted sound reached into Archer's chest with a surge of warmth. "Hi, I'm Sandy from DHS. A little roasted and toasted."

More warmth surged through him. He liked her self-deprecating humor. He liked her…a lot. She got him. But good. After the mission, he was going to do something he hadn't done in decades. Date. He was going to ask her out on a proper—get dressed in fancy clothes—date, with plenty more to follow. Given her responses to him, like the way chemistry had exploded between them five minutes ago, and she softened in his arms, he'd say his chances were good she'd say yes. The main obstacle he saw was her son. Hopefully, Brian wouldn't have an issue with a retired SEAL dating his mother.

Archer waved his hand toward the couple stocking the cupboards. "That's Bella and Matteo Santarelli. Like TJ, they work for the Knight Agency."

"Except, I work out of D.C. and they work out of Atlantic City," TJ said between bites.

Sandy nodded at the hacker then turned to the couple. "You two are married?"

Bella stepped forward to shake hands. "Yes, I finally broke down and made an honest man of him.

And I'm *really* hoping you've found us some terrorists to hunt. I'm going through withdrawal."

"Well, whoever they are, they just tried to barbeque me because of what we must've stumbled onto yesterday," Sandy said, and his insides fisted tight as an image of her stuck in that burning room while he couldn't do a goddam thing flashed through his mind. "So, they're bad. Does that count?"

Bella released Sandy's hand and grinned. "Absolutely."

"We're glad you're okay," Matteo said, stepping forward to shake Sandy's hand and slip an arm around Bella. The man was a former SEAL Archer had the pleasure to command several years ago. "Don't mind my wife. She hasn't emptied her gun in anyone lately. She'll feel better when she can draw her weapon."

"Yes." Bella nodded, sliding her arm around her husband while reaching for pizza with her free hand. "Any weapon. Gun. Blade. I don't care. Just give me someone to bring down."

Sandy laughed again. "I'll do my best."

He could tell she thought the woman was just being funny, but she wasn't. Bella "Banshee" Monroe Santerelli was a former terrorist hunter for a secret government unit, and a hell of a good one. Archer's SEAL team had worked with her once in Islamabad. Their job had been to get her inside a fortress, provide backup, and grab all the electronics. By the time they'd secured every laptop and hard drive in the place, Bella had taken out fourteen guards and two top-level ISIS heavy hitters upstairs. When he'd gotten back to base later, he watched the com footage, impressed as hell at the way she'd cut through the enemy like butter. Her moves were symmetric, almost like a well-timed waltz. Only a motivated, determined woman would move that way. Someone who wanted to wipe all terrorists off the face of the earth.

He was on board with that.

He also understood how a person that driven would go stir-crazy working in the private sector. She needed a target, but he couldn't provide that yet. And although they were dealing with people willing to kill to keep their identity a secret, Archer wasn't yet convinced it was terrorists. More investigating and digging were required. As well as more recon.

"This pizza's good," Bella said, before glancing up at Matteo. "Not as delicious as yours, honey. But definitely some of the best I've tasted in New York."

The former SEAL nodded after finishing his second slice. "I agree. It's good."

Between cases, Matteo helped at the pizza shop his father owned on the boardwalk in Atlantic City. Archer ate there often.

He understood his friend's desire to keep an eye on his dad. Keep him safe. Archer felt the same about his mother. Right about now, she and her sister were on a private jet, courtesy of Jameson, on her way to a private resort off the coast of Florida, also courtesy of Jameson, for her early birthday present, courtesy of him. Archer wanted her off the grid and nowhere near the city until the mission was over. If his cover was somehow blown, he wouldn't have to worry about her safety.

"Well, Sandy," TJ said, nodding toward her bag behind her. "I see you've brought your laptop. I'm ready to get cracking on whatever you need me to do whenever you are."

Archer straightened. "After she has the chance to shower and change."

She sighed. "That'd be great. Both offers."

She divided her smile between him and TJ, and Archer's insides fisted tight for an entirely different reason this time. His muddled brain mixed up her meaning, and the thought of offering to take a shower with the sexy woman was enough to cause more than his tongue to swell.

"But someone wouldn't allow me to go home to fetch clean clothes." She looked pointedly at him.

"No worries." Bella grinned. "Archer asked me to stop and pick up a few things for you on our way in from Jersey. The bags are in your room upstairs. First door on the right."

"Oh." Sandy blinked. "I thought you'd just arrived."

Bella shook her head. "Nope. Stopped in, dropped stuff off, then as TJ said, made a supply run."

"Oh," Sandy repeated, then frowned. "How'd you know my size?"

A wide smile spread across the other woman's face. "Archer told me."

Shit.

Color rose up into Sandy's cheeks, as she slowly met his gaze. "You did?"

He opened his mouth to tell her he hadn't, but Bella beat him to it.

"Just kidding," the woman said, grin still in place. "It was in your file."

Sandy's brows shot up. "They have my measurements in my file?"

"No." Bella shook her head. "I went off your height and weight and your photo."

"Oh," Sandy said for the third time. "Sorry. Guess my mind is still befuddled from the smoke."

Concern sliced through him, straightening his spine. "Is anything else bothering you? Maybe I should get you to the ER."

"No. I'm fine," she rushed to say. "I just need that shower and to change, and I'll be good as new. So, if you could point me to my room and the bathroom, I'll get going."

"Come on. I'll show you," Bella said, and Archer watched the two women head for the stairs. "Each room has its own bathroom, so you don't have to worry about sharing." Bella glanced at him while she climbed the stairs. "Unless you want to."

Jesus, the woman was pushing it.

Matteo's chuckle met his ears. "Sorry, sir. My wife's in rare form today."

He grunted, "I'd ask you to try to rein her in, but I know that's folly."

This time TJ laughed. "That'd be like trying to wrangle a feral cat."

The three of them nodded at the accurate analogy.

"So, what's your take on things? Do you have a game plan?" Matteo asked, leaning against the sink, arms folded across his chest.

"Yes." He nodded. "We've reconned the outside of the bank. Now it's time to recon the inside."

CHAPTER EIGHT

Later that night, Sandy sat in what TJ called his "cyber sanctuary", watching Archer, Matteo, and Bella working their way through every floor of the World Bank while efficiently avoiding security. If she hadn't had a pounding headache, she might've thought it was dream, because...well, that was insane. So was the fact the three were setting up cameras and com links.

"Why are they necessary if you've hacked into the system?" she asked.

TJ glanced over at her and shrugged. "Insurance."

She frowned. "For what?"

"In case this is that ghost group from Munich."

She had no idea what he was talking about. "What group?"

His chin lifted, and he hit a few buttons that brought up a feed on one of his eight monitors of a bombing several years ago. She remembered it was a brewery or museum, and innocent tourists had been killed.

"Their MO is to cut electricity before they strike."

"Oh." She nodded. "Insurance." Now they had video access regardless.

TJ drummed on the console with his index fingers and grinned. "Exactly."

Her heart rocked as a thought occurred. "What if the perpetrators are tapped into the feed and watching Archer and the others right now?"

The guy grinned, running a hand through his wavy red hair. "That's the beauty of being me. I have the output running on a loop, so anyone watching won't see a thing. But I can watch in real time here." He pointed to a monitor. "No one's the wiser."

"Brilliant."

He grinned. "I know."

Sandy laughed. "Humble, too."

He shrugged before he nodded to the bombing footage. "It's possible you captured someone's face yesterday that was involved in that."

Yesterday's photo shoot immediately played through her mind. The only one who stood out was the eye tattoo guy, but she knew most of the time it was never the obvious person. More often than not, the perpetrators were usually the ones who liked to blend in.

"Hopefully, the facial recognition software will ID Mr. Clean." TJ nodded to the monitor that was running a photo of the guy through the program. Luckily, her phone had been deemed safe after TJ examined it and added some special safeguards. He did the same with her laptop. Even though she didn't really know the hacker, she felt safer using her electronics now. Safe enough to contact her son, who was currently between assignments.

Earlier in the evening, she'd spent a half hour FaceTiming with Brian. When he asked where she was because her bedroom here definitely lacked the warmth of her house, and was too dark to pass as her office, she simply told him on assignment. With whom and why were never brought up. Her son knew she wouldn't, and couldn't, disclose those details. And she certainly wouldn't tell him about the fire that morning.

"TJ, I was wondering," she said. "If my phone wasn't tampered with, how did someone text Archer making it appear to come from it?"

Anger removed the amusement from his face. "There is software out there available on the dark web the bad guys can use to do exactly that."

"So, they used it on my boss too, to make him think Archer hadn't wanted him in that meeting."

TJ shrugged. "Possibly. I'd have to examine his phone to be sure."

No need. Sandy was sure, even though she knew Archer still had suspicions. That was okay. She understood why he would. But she knew better and chose to spend her time looking for the real mole.

"Find any unauthorized entry?" she asked, nodding to the DHS feed Silas had secured for them earlier. She hated to think another coworker had deliberately set her up, but she wasn't naive. There were plenty of reasons to cause even the most dedicated person to turn.

"Nada." He drummed the console with one hand. "But, I will."

"Want some help?"

He grinned and pushed off the console to propel his chair to the right to make room for hers. "Absolutely. Come join the party."

She rolled her chair closer, and together, they spent the next hour scouring footage. No one other than Dave had gone in today, and everyone they watched using the keypad to access the room yesterday had reason to be in there.

Several agents, two secretaries setting up for a meeting, then that meeting involving a group of five people, two higher ups, the receptionist bringing in files, the maintenance man, who according to the log, had fixed the thermostat, and Dave again, in with his boss. Thanks to the no camera policy in the meeting room, a safeguard to prevent being hacked, there was no way to see who did what in the room.

The precaution had backfired.

She'd gotten the distinct impression someone other than Archer had been watching her. The timing of the lights going out when her attention had focused on busting the wall was too coincidental. She didn't believe in them. Now, the lack of feed had made it easy for the bomber to act undetected.

It only amped up her determination to uncover the culprit.

She kept at it for several hours, staying up long after the others had returned and retired for the night. There was something she was missing. She could feel it but dammit, her brain was just too worn out to properly function.

Claiming the same thing, TJ yawned and got up to stretch out on a cot set up along the wall. "Go grab a few hours of shut eye, Sandy. I've learned it's the best way to let your brain recharge." He yawned again. "I'll meet you back here in the morning."

Although she wanted to continue, Sandy understood the merit of his suggestion. Her brain did need the break. And her body, too. It'd been a taxing day, both mentally and physically. So she headed to her room, stripped out of the clothes Bella had brought—which fit perfectly—and into the nightshirt that had been among the purchases. And surprisingly, within minutes of slipping between the sheets, Sandy fell asleep.

Despite going to bed late, she was in the kitchen early the next morning, filling a mug with coffee when Bella sauntered down the stairs and ambled toward her. "I thought I smelled coffee."

She smiled. "I'm not the one responsible, but it called to me, too." The pot had already been brewed before she'd arrived.

"Archer, no doubt. He's probably in the sanctuary with TJ," Bella said, reaching for a mug from a cupboard, her long, brown hair wet, her posture relaxed, her expression...satisfied. "I left Matteo upstairs to finish showering, so I know it wasn't him."

She remembered sharing morning showers with her late husband. It wasn't just the sex she missed from being in a relationship, it was the companionship, the fun, the unspoken support. Nate had been one of those one-in-a-million men. Special. And she hadn't met anyone even remotely close...until Archer.

Without any effort, the seasoned SEAL had gotten past the debris and booby traps and clutter she'd accumulated around her heart over the past two decades. They had a connection. He got her. Made her feel good with just his presence. Made her want to soothe away the shadows she sometimes saw in his eyes. Ease the pain he harbored deep inside. Make him feel whole. It was all-powerful, unexpected, and quick. Damn quick.

It scared the hell out of her and excited her at the same time.

"...a good man," Bella said.

Sandy blinked and set her cup on the counter. "What?" Her mind had been elsewhere, so she had no idea what she'd missed from the conversation.

"Archer. He's a good man." Bella's grin broadened as the heat in Sandy's face increased. "He adores you. And it's as plain as the blush on your face that you have feelings for him."

He adored her?

Perhaps. It wasn't like they'd just met. They'd known each other socially and infrequently for several years now.

But...adored?

Warmth spread through her at the thought, lingering in her chest. What should she do about it? Was it even worth contemplating?

"Yes, it is," Bella said as if reading her mind. "Not long ago, I stood in your shoes, at a similar crossroads, and I'm glad I chose the hard road. The one that required the leap of faith."

"But the job..."

"Is just a job. It has nothing to do with how you feel about each other...other than to make you realize *how* you feel about each other." The brunette set her cup down and folded her arms across her chest. "You should've seen Archer yesterday, when he had no idea what had happened to you in that burning room. He was determined to get to you at all costs. It didn't matter what he had to go through—or who—he was going to find you. Trust me, when it's personal, you'll do whatever it takes to get the job done. When your heart is involved, it makes you unstoppable...and *that's* the Archer I saw yesterday. Does he adore you? Very much."

Well...wow.

Sandy slumped against the counter and set a hand over her heart to keep the thudding thing from bursting through her chest. "But we don't really know each other."

"Time will take care of that." The pretty agent smiled and sipped her coffee.

Since she had no response to that, Sandy reached for her forgotten mug and finished her coffee. It was way too early in the morning for her to contemplate a subject so involving and intriguing as Archer, without more caffeine.

"How does a mother of a SEAL become an analyst for DHS?" Bella asked. "Is it something you always strived to do?"

She smiled. "No. It all started when I worked for the DA's office. I was originally hired as a secretary, but on this one case, I'd noticed a pattern—a connection to three seemingly unrelated crimes. I pointed it out, they investigated, and discovered I was right. After that, I was part of their investigation team." It'd been an amazing ten years. "I really enjoyed it."

"Why'd you leave?"

"Because of the Sisterhood."

Bella's brows rose. "You mean in the CIA? The analysts who found Bin Laden?"

"Yes. From the Alec Station Unit." Sandy smiled. Most people didn't know about the team authorized by President Clinton to track down Bin Laden back in 1995. "You know about them?"

"Hell, yeah." Bella nodded. "Those women were amazing. Some of them still analyze chatter and supply the intel to my old unit. I heard the man who created the team said half of the applicants had been women, and after working with them, he'd wished they'd all been women."

She nodded again. Those women were her heroes and the reason she did what she did today. "Between May of '98 and '99 they found Bin Laden ten different times, working up two missions to capture him and eight different missions to take him down."

Bella whistled. "Jesus, what happened?"

"That's what I'd like to know," Archer growled, causing Sandy to jump. She turned to find him leaning against the wall by the hall that led to the sanctuary. "Why the hell was that man still alive in 2001?"

Her heart rocked in her chest and pulse pounded loudly in her ears. She knew what he'd lost and could've kicked herself for not holding this conversation with Bella in private. It was too late, now, though. She cleared her throat. "White House administration. It was deemed too risky. They didn't want to cause an international incident."

Archer blew out a breath and shook his head.

The Sisterhood had found him again. Several times, in fact. It'd been green-lit by Clinton again, but winter had set in and the mission had been put on hold until the spring. But by then, it was a new president with a new administration who canceled the mission.

Later that year...the towers fell.

"They persevered, though." She raised her chin. "For seventeen years, they tracked him down, worked up missions, dealt with rejection, several presidential administrations, until they were asked to find him again, and when they did, they wrote up a mission that was green-lit, finally carried out, and successful."

Archer walked over to refill his mug. "I can see you admire them. So...why aren't you working for the CIA?"

She shrugged. "Good question. They'd tried to recruit me at the same time DHS did, but...I don't know...I went with my gut."

Working out of Langley would've put her much closer to her son, but something told her to accept Homeland's offer.

Archer set the carafe back in the coffee maker and met her gaze. "Perhaps it boils down to this mission."

Bella nodded behind him, cupping her mug with both hands. "Fate."

A shiver raced down Sandy's spine.

Could the woman be right?

***

Archer wasn't sure about fate, but he knew not to question it. His mind was still trying to process the bomb Sandy had dropped about the CIA having had the opportunity to take down Bin Laden before 2001.

Damn bureaucratic bullshit.

He clenched his jaw and rode out the wave of nausea. One good thing about retirement was not having to deal with it. All the jobs he did for the Knight Agency fell into the *not having to deal with it* category. Jameson was a former SOG operative with the CIA, so he accepted work for his agency that flew under the government's radar.

This job for Silas, however, was government sanctioned, which meant it was monitored. But so far, he wasn't working with his hands tied, and didn't regret it.

His gaze slid up the sweet, yawning blonde, mainlining her coffee like it was about to disappear. She wore a pair of jeans that hugged her curves to perfection, a bubblegum pink scoop neck shirt that teased him with a peek of cleavage and messed with his pulse. Her hair was piled on her head in that haphazard bun again, with pieces hanging free to brush her face and neck, making him itch to touch her soft skin.

So, he finished his coffee and made another pot. He was going to need it.

Two hours later, he rose from his chair in the sanctuary and stretched the kinks out of his back. So far, their recon had amassed nothing. He and Sandy were viewing the DHS feed from yesterday. The audio mingled in the air with the live feed from the bank Matteo and Bella were viewing, and TJ worked in the middle, hacking into DHS per Archer's request that morning.

He knew he could run it by Silas and that it might be granted, but it was always better to ask forgiveness than permission. And since Sandy's life had been threatened, he wasn't about to chance getting caught in that bureaucratic red tape shit.

"So, Sandy, I was wondering," TJ said, tipping his head sideways as he looked at her. "Can you do Sherlock Holmes-type evaluations on people at a glance?"

Her lips twitched. "I suppose. Why?"

"Let's see what you got." TJ folded his arms across his chest and smiled at her. "What did I do today?"

"Dude." Bella smirked. "She's been in here with you all morning."

TJ frowned. "Not the whole time."

Sandy sat back in her chair and chewed her lower lip while regarding the red-headed motor mouth thoughtfully.

Heat skittered through Archer, overcome with the sudden urge to soothe her lip with his tongue. Inhaling deeply, he removed his gaze from her lips and focused on TJ instead. They had work to do, but he knew the merits of allowing his team a little break. Besides, he was curious to see what Sandy could do.

"You slept in your clothes," she said. "Nuked a burrito for breakfast, washed it down with peach iced tea, then washed that down with an energy drink. Ran your left hand through your hair because you have a paper cut on a finger on your right hand. And you finished hacking into DHS ten minutes ago but have yet to tell Archer."

The kid sat up, while his jaw dropped. "How the hell…?"

"You mean she's right?" Matteo asked, smile quirking his lips.

"Yeah, and she wasn't around for the burrito and drinks." He blinked at Sandy. "How'd you know about my cut? And all of it?"

She laughed. "I don't know. It's just stuff that I see clearly. Like the burrito wrapper and empty drink bottles in the trash by your leg. That's no biggie."

"And the cut?" He held up his right index finger. "How'd you know? You can't really see it and I'm not wearing a band-aid."

"True, but you *are* wearing glue from it." She shrugged. "Stuff anyone can see."

Son-of-a-bitch.

Archer frowned at the kid's finger. TJ did have a faint glue line.

"But how'd you know I didn't run it through my hair?

"Because your right side isn't as messy as your left," she said simply.

Archer knew everything she was saying was mostly gleaned from common sense, but most people would never pick up on it. He'd caught some, but the glue line? He never would've picked up on that.

"And the DHS hacking?" TJ asked. "How'd you know I'd finished?"

She smiled outright, and Archer *felt* it in his chest like a burst of warmth. "Because you started drumming on the console ten minutes ago. When you're working, all ten of your fingers are busy clicking keys at crazy speeds."

TJ stretched out then folded his hands behind his head, smug smile on his face. "True. I've burned through many keyboards with my strokes."

Archer snickered. The hacker was twenty-six but appeared nineteen. Regardless, he was damn good at his job. He'd have to be, for Jameson to employ the MIT graduate and get the guy's Federal prison record expunged.

"That was amazing, Sandy." Bella stood up and waved at her body. "Do me next."

Sandy opened her mouth, then stilled a second before she pointed to a monitor near Matteo. "TJ, quick…isolate that feed and record it."

The kid frowned but did as directed, his fingers flying over two different keyboards at the same time. "Done."

"What is it?" he asked, eyeing the bank employee sitting behind a desk, talking to another employee in the same room.

"Hang on." Sandy pulled her laptop out of her bag by her feet, and once it booted up, she signed on and scrolled through files within folders. "I've heard him before. Find out who he is," she said, clicking on something that opened an audio file. She slid the headphone jack into a port on her laptop, shoved the headphones on her head and listened to the file. A second later, she glanced up at him, her face lighting up as she nodded. "It is him." Her gaze shifted to TJ. "I'm going to send it to you so you can verify. Give me your email." She shoved the laptop to TJ who typed in his address, she attached the file and hit send.

"Got it," TJ said, his fingers tapping the keys on two keyboards again, and on one of the monitors in front of him, the voice samples overlap. "She's right. It's the same guy."

Archer worked to keep his hope in check. "Sandy, where did you get your audio?"

"It's from last week's chatter," she said. "It's part of the reason we're all here."

TJ flicked a switch and the audio filled the room. The tone did sound similar, but the man was speaking Punjabi, not English.

Damn…she had a hell of an ear.

Finally, they had their first lead. Their first viable suspect.

"What's he saying?" TJ asked, as he glanced at everyone's frowning faces. "I can see I'm the only one who doesn't know."

Sandy sighed. "Basically, capitalist pigs will be sorry. They will pay."

Archer grit his teeth over the *"Death to Americans"* part she'd left out.

Not on his watch.

"How the hell did you remember that from all those files you listen to?" TJ asked, nodding toward her laptop.

Sandy shrugged. "When someone threatens my country, it sort of sticks in my head."

"Great catch." Bella cracked her knuckles, then set a hand on TJ's shoulder. "Now, how about we get this guy's address so I can pay him a visit."

Shit. Archer stiffened. He had to keep an eye on that one. He didn't like the smile on her face.

"We need him alive, Bella," he felt compelled to spell out. "We have to find out exactly who we're dealing with and what they have planned.

The woman's expression dimmed. "Spoil sport. How about *after* we squeeze information out of him?"

"Calm down, sweetheart," Matteo said, stroking Bella's back. "Let Archer do his job. You know he'll throw you scraps."

Bella blew out a breath, relaxed her fist, and nodded. "Okay. I can wait."

"Are you going to pay him a visit at the bank?" TJ asked.

As much as Archer wanted to go there and drag the guy out by his scrawny little neck, he shook his head. "No. He's not the boss." He studied the man on the live feed. The guy sat with his chest puffed out, which was usually a signal for underlying insecurities. Not something a man in charge would do. Straight shoulders, wide stance, eye contact—yes—but not a puffed-out chest. "He's a follower, so we'll let him lead us to his leader."

"Sweet." TJ grinned. "That means stakeout time."

"But get me his address," Archer said. "Find out his hours and if he drives to work. Or takes the subway. Cab. Uber. If so, which ones?"

"On it, boss." Idiot saluted him before spinning back around to clack at the keys.

"Better hurry with that info, TJ," Matteo said, pointing to the screen. "Looks like we have a rabbit."

The kid frowned. "A what?"

"Rabbit," Matteo repeated. "He shut down his computer. Grabbed his jacket, briefcase, and pushed his chair in. He's leaving."

Dammit.

They were twenty-five minutes away from the bank on a good traffic day. They'd never get there before he left.

"Looks like we're going to have to visit his home. Text me his address," he told TJ. "And whatever else you dig up about him. Bella, Matteo, you're with me."

"Done," TJ said.

Sandy fished her purse out of her laptop case and straightened.

"No." He shook his head. "You stay with TJ and continue to go through the tapes."

"Think I'd be more help with you," she said, slipping the purse across her body. "What if you find him having dinner with some of his friends?"

He narrowed his eyes and cocked his head. "Then we'll wait until they leave before making our move."

She shook her head. "What if one or more of those *friends* are in my files, too?"

Damn…that was possible. "Then TJ can give me equipment so you can listen in and tell us which ones are of interest."

He was *not* taking that woman outside and exposing her to danger.

No way.

"What if it's someone in the lobby?" she continued, "Or on the street? Or—"

Shit. "All right." He held up a hand and blew out a breath. "You can come. Just stick close."

"Any chance we can swing by my place so I can get my gun?" she asked, and he wondered if she was trying to stop his heart.

He shook his head. "You won't need one."

"And if you do, you can have one of mine," Bella said, strapping a knife to her ankle...next to a gun. "I prefer to use a blade, anyway."

He turned to Sandy. "See? If you need a gun, you can use one of Bella's."

Over his dead body, but neither woman needed to know.

CHAPTER NINE

Sandy couldn't believe Archer actually let her tag along. She still stood by her argument. She needed to be with them to case out the people nearby, but hadn't really expected the stubborn man to give in.

The address TJ texted was in north Brooklyn, near the Navy yards. They might've caught a break. It depended on the suspect's mode of transportation and the route he took to get home.

If he was going home.

They decided to assume he was and rushed from south Brooklyn to meet the guy there.

According to TJ, they were looking for James Rowlands, who lived on the fourth floor of an apartment building on Bridge Street.

Archer parked on the street, cut the engine and turned to face her. "Stick close to me."

She nodded. For some reason, he thought she was a rookie. She wasn't a seasoned agent, but Sandy had been hitting the streets since her DA days. This was no different. If she sensed trouble, she knew enough to stay out of it and call it in…which in this case, meant letting them handle it.

"And you," Archer said, transferring his gaze to Bella, sitting behind Sandy, "don't kill anyone."

"Got ya. Maim, don't kill," came Bella's quick reply.

Sandy bit her bottom lip to keep from laughing. It wasn't funny, except it was...until she caught Archer's stone-faced expression. Her mirth died a quick death. She opened her door and exited the vehicle. Thankfully, they'd left her SUV behind and took the black one she was told was registered to the Knight Agency.

"Keep your eyes and ears peeled," Archer said, joining her on the sidewalk, then shocked her by slipping his arm around her.

She noted Matteo had done the same with Bella. Guess they were going with the couple's persona. The other two actually were a couple, but it made sense to carry on the ruse. Over the years, Sandy had noted that often times public shows of affection made others uncomfortable and they tended not to look your way. It could come in handy today.

They entered the lobby of the apartment building, finding it mostly vacant. The concierge stood behind a counter on their left. Matteo and Bella went over to talk with him. A middle-aged man sat on a couch reading a newspaper and another, older man sat in a corner reading a book. Neither looked up at them. A woman with an infant in one hand and a two year old holding her pants leg was checking her mailbox beyond the concierge. To their right was a small coffee shop with three patrons, one of them very familiar.

"Sandy?" The man smiled and stepped toward them.

She released Archer and moved to intercept one of her old informants so their impending conversation wouldn't be heard by those in the lobby. "Stan, how are you?"

Perhaps today was her lucky day.

"I'm good, you know? Life has its ups and downs, and right now I'm riding the up side." He winked, pulling her in for a quick hug before releasing her. "'Bout time you gots yourself a boyfriend." He nodded to Archer, who'd joined them, setting his hand on her back.

She introduced them and tried to prevent color from her rising into her face. She failed. Luckily, it worked for their charade. "Do you live here?" she asked, to change the subject and because she was curious. This building wasn't as nice as hers, but it was a heck of a lot better than the places Stan used to dwell.

Plus, it could help their mission.

He nodded. "Second floor, corner with a nice view of the city over the river. I recently came into some money that was owed me from disability, so I gots me this place." The man was a Caucasian in his mid-forties but living a hard life had aged him. "Heard you're no longer DA, but Uncle Sam now," he said, keeping his voice low, and the smile on his face. "So, what brings you here? Business or pleasure? And I really hope it's pleasure because it can't be good if it's business."

She glanced at Archer, who gave her a small nod. "Business," she replied, and motioned with a wave of her hand to a table where they sat while

Archer went to fetch coffees to keep a normal appearance. "Do you know James Rowlands?"

Stan furrowed his weathered brows, turning his deep wrinkles into a ravine. "The fancy dressed dude from four-fifteen? He's quiet but he don't make no eye contact." Stan grimaced. "I don't like no one who don't make no eye contact. They's hiding something."

A correct observation. "Does he get visitors?" she asked

Archer returned with their drinks and sat between them at the small, high table, effectively using his large body to block their conversation from any onlookers behind him.

"Every Tuesday at three, *even* if Jimmy is still at work. I call him Jimmy because I think he'd hate it." Stan grinned, showing off all four of his teeth.

"How do you know it's every Tuesday at three?" Archer asked before sipping his coffee.

"Because me and Bobby Granger, we play checkers at three every day in his apartment across the hall in four-sixteen, and sometimes I sees the stuffy, unsmiling suits on Tuesdays in the elevator on my way up."

Archer set his cup on the table and glanced at Stan. "Any idea how long they stay?"

"No, sir." Stan shook his head. "Sometimes me and Bobby...we enjoy us a little too much hooch and I don't get back to my place until the next day. Sorry."

While Archer and Stan had been talking, she carefully opened her purse under the table. All she'd had on her was two twenty dollar bills and some ones, so she rolled them up and concealed it in her palm. "It's okay,' she said, reaching out to pat Stan's hand and slid the money under his palm. "You've been very helpful. Thank you."

"Anytime." He grinned. "It's always nice catch up with a friend."

She left the table with Archer, glancing around to see if anyone watched, but the scene hadn't changed, other than the mother with two children by the mailboxes had disappeared. "Well?" she asked Archer quietly as they made their way across the lobby toward Bella and Matteo standing near the elevators. "What do you think the meetings are about?"

"I don't know, but aim to find out," he said.

"Who was your friend?" Bella asked when they neared.

She rezipped her purse. "An old informant from my DA days."

"Did he have anything helpful to say?" Matteo asked.

Archer filled them in, then pressed the up button. "We'll use the elevator, you two take the stairs."

Happy to be part of the elevator crew, Sandy stood quietly next to Archer, waiting for him to ask her to remain in the hall. Oh, she knew it was coming. She could tell by the way his jaw worked as he clenched and unclenched his teeth. The way his breathing increased and he wouldn't meet her gaze...all signs that he had something on his mind, knew she wouldn't like it, but he needed to figure out what kind of spin to put on it so she'd comply.

He lifted his chin and appeared to watch the lighted floors tick by. "When we get to Rowland's apartment, I want you to stay in the hall."

She snickered.

"It isn't funny." He turned and stepped close, forcing her to move until her back hit the wall.

Anger pricked at her spine. Strong-arming was the wrong tactic to use on her. "I never said it was."

"I don't want any flack on this, Sandy," he said. "We didn't have proper time to surveille the place. Investigate him, his acquaintances, his neighbors. I don't like going in unprepared, but I don't feel we have a choice. And TJ hasn't picked the guy up on any cameras, so we don't know if he's home or if there are others." Archer lifted a hand to gently graze her cheek with the back of his knuckles. "I refuse to take any chances with you. I won't do it."

The concern in his eyes and his touch sucked the fight right out of her. "Okay."

He blinked at her. "Okay?"

"Yeah..." She nodded, a little surprised, too, but she wasn't exactly thrilled to go inside without a weapon anyway, so she'd play it his way. For now. "I'll wait in the hall until you clear the apartment, but then I'm coming in."

He nodded, brushing his thumb over her lower lip. "Deal."

It was a good thing the elevator stopped because her body wanted to press into his, but the doors opened, and they stepped out—separately—and joined Bella and Matteo standing outside the apartment in question.

True to her word, Sandy waited outside while the other three knocked then entered. She heard a mild skirmish, the scrape of chair legs against floor, then a crash and an, "umph". When things quieted down, Sandy peeked inside the opened door to find a lamp smashed on the floor, a chair upturned, and James Rowlands sitting on another with his hands zip-tied behind his back.

But what really caught her eye was the map spread out on the kitchen table. A map of the streets around the Federal Reserve Bank of New York.

"Why the map? You don't know how to find your way to work?" The questions were out before she could stop them.

Bella and Matteo snickered, Archer raised a brow and one of his dimples threatened to appear.

Rowlands however, sneered at Bella and her. "None of your business, you stupid bitches," he spouted in Punjabi.

Archer's face turned red, his mouth disappeared into a thin line, and he raised a fist that shook…but it was Bella's fist that made contact with Rowland's face.

Twice.

"Sorry, boss," the pretty agent said. "But you did say you didn't want him dead. *Yet*. And I wasn't sure your fist knew the difference between maim and kill."

Archer's top lip curled, and his jaw cracked, but he relaxed his fist and nodded. "Thanks."

"Now, listen, Jimmy," Bella said in Punjabi, patting the guy's bruised face none-to-gently. "If you're going to insult us, then you need to get it right. It's stupid *American* bitches. Got it?"

After Sandy fist-bumped Bella's fist in a TJ maneuver, they began to investigate while the men interrogated Rowlands.

She checked out the bedroom, Bella took the bathroom, then they met back in the hall. "Bedroom's clean. Nothing out of the ordinary."

"Bathroom's disgusting." Bella gagged. "But clear."

They worked their way through the kitchen and living room, and other than that map, nothing stood out. But there was something there. Sandy could feel it. So, she stood off to the side and watched the man as the former SEALs interrogated him.

Ten minutes later, and a puddle of pee under his chair, the guy remained silent. He did, however, keep glancing toward the books in the bookcase in the far corner. Sandy watched him, as she slowly walked to it. His chest rose quicker. She examined the books, but the dust in front of them signaled they hadn't been touched recently. Then she noticed the scuff marks on the floor, and her heart rocked.

"Uh…Archer? Matteo?" She motioned for them to join her. This part required muscle, which those men had in spades. "We need to move this bookcase."

She stepped out of the way and watched as the men inspected the area, deeming it free of booby traps before moving it in the direction of the scuff marks.

"Son-of-a-bitch…"

"Shit."

The men's expletives echoed one another as they stared into a small, hidden closet full of guns, ammo, and an empty crate marked *detonators*. Damn. That meant someone was running around New York City with a bunch of detonators *and* obviously the bombs to go with them.

She was just about to ask what their next move was when the door opened and a guy in black jeans, black sneakers, and gray hoodie walked in. He took one look at James, then glanced at them, before he pivoted around and shot out the door.

Sandy followed, with Archer grumbling behind her to stand down.

The guy ran down the hall, shoulder-checking poor Stan, who'd exited the elevator at the wrong time. He fell backward into the closed doors, but righted himself, telling them he was okay as they ran past.

Expecting the hoodie to take a left and head for the stairs, Sandy was shocked when the guy ran full speed at the window at the end of the hall and charged shoulder-first, straight through it.

Panting, she stopped, expecting to see a body on the ground, but only glass and wood from the window pane littered the pavement. The culprit was on a fire escape attached to the building across the alley, climbing his way down.

"Move," Bella called, and running full-force, she, too, jumped out the window, landing on the same fire escape the perpetrator had just vacated.

Holy… "She just…she just jumped out the window."

"I know." He nodded. "She's a freerunner. Came in handy when she used to hunt terrorists."

"Ah…she knows parkour." A training discipline Sandy had heard about. It was developed from military obstacle course training. Which meant Bella could get from one point to another without equipment assistance in the fastest, most efficient way possible. Like jumping out of a window instead of taking the stairs. That explained why the capable agent followed the suspect. "Should we go help?"

Archer glanced out the window, no doubt noting Bella already had the guy face down against the pavement with her knee in his back while zip-tying his wrists. "No. I'd say she's got that one covered."

"Sandy," Stan stumbled close, holding his stomach. "I…why am I…bleeding?" he asked, holding out his hands, blood dripping from his fingers onto the floor before he started to sway.

Her heart rolled into her ribs. The guy in the gray hoodie…

Archer lunged forward and caught Stan and helped him to lay flat. He glanced up at her. "He's been stabbed. Call 911."

***

Archer lost track of time. It could've been two hours, it could've been ten, by the time he and Sandy emerged from the hospital. It came as no surprise when she'd insisted on going with Stan and waiting until surgery was over, and Archer wasn't about to leave her side, other than to go grab some cheap souvenir T-shirts from a store down the block to replace their bloody clothing.

After a quick change in the restrooms, they headed outside, and he was surprised to see it was still light outside. He pulled out his phone and noted it was just past five. "I'll call Bella to pick us up." He wasn't comfortable having Matteo fetch them, while leaving the overzealous agent to watch over their two prisoners alone.

Especially since one of their prisoners had stabbed poor Stan in the ribs. A little higher and to the left, and he would've caught the guy's heart. Luckily, the man hadn't lost too much blood—thanks to Sandy keeping pressure on the wound until the paramedics had arrived, while he'd been busy coordinating the extraction of the two possible terrorists and all the contents in that damn closet. He was eager to get back to headquarters to see what, if anything, they'd uncovered.

"Wait," Sandy said, placing a hand on his wrist. "It's still early yet. I'd like to head to DHS. There's a file on my desktop that could help." She paused and looked around then met his gaze again. "I just think we should get it."

So, one Uber ride and twenty minutes later, they exited the car and stood in front of DHS headquarters. His mind was transported back to watching that damn room burning with Sandy trapped inside, when he heard someone calling out her name.

"Look, it's Rodrigo," she said, pointing to a nearby hot dog cart. She released him to walk over to the young man.

The vendor's face lit up. "Ms. Sandy, how are you enjoying your trip to the Big Apple?"

"It's great." She smiled. "How are you? I didn't realize you could move your stand around the city."

The young man laughed. "Yeah. As long as we have a license." He pointed to the license hanging on his cart. "And go where vending is allowed, and don't encroach on someone's territory. That could get your tires slashed."

Sandy frowned. "That's awful."

Archer joined her, silently listening to the exchange.

Rodrigo shrugged. "Could be worse. So...can I get you one with mustard, two with ketchup?"

"Sure." She turned to him and smiled. "You're up for another two, right?"

Both impressed and alarmed the guy remembered their orders, he grinned to keep up appearances. "Always."

His mind raced. There were over three thousand independent vendors in the city, and twice, within three days—at two different locations—they run into the same guy? Way too suspect for him.

As he paid for the dogs, he made a mental note to have TJ double-check the man's license and ID again. After bidding the vendor farewell, they walked across the small courtyard in front of the building's entrance, polishing off their food by the time they reached the doors.

"The least amount of time we spend in here, the better," he said, opening the door for her when she nodded.

Getting in wasn't much of a hassle. Sandy had her credentials and he just had to fill out a form for a visitor pass. The elevator opened as they neared, and her boss stepped out.

"Hi, Sandy." He appeared genuinely pleased to see her. "I didn't know you were coming in."

She shrugged. "Need something from my desk. I'm not staying long."

"Mr. Monroe." Dave nodded, appearing genuinely *not* pleased to see Archer.

He nodded back. "Webster."

"Have a good night," the man said, then disappeared into the exiting crowd.

After that, the majority of the building was quiet. The normal workforce had gone for the day. He attributed that to their non-stop elevator ride. In silence. He liked how Sandy seemed to be on the same page as him, without discussing it. She instinctively knew to keep the chatter to a minimum.

When they got out on her floor, she greeted the receptionist who was packing up her purse as if getting ready to leave for the day.

The woman glanced up and smiled. "Sandy...glad to see you're okay."

"Me, too." Sandy grinned.

"Oh, wait. You'll need this to get in your new door." The woman hurried around the desk to drop a key in Sandy's hand. "It had to be replaced."

"Oh, okay. Thanks, Amy," Sandy said, her jaw working as if trying to keep from laughing. "Wonder why it needed replacing?" she muttered under her breath for only his ears.

He held back a grin as she led him down to the office he'd pretty much ransacked yesterday when she'd sent him in for her laptop and purse. "Looks like they still need to fix your drawer, though."

"Wow, you...ah...did that?" She looked from the bent top drawer sitting on her desk to him and blinked. "You're SEAL strong."

"Hooyah."

She smiled. "Hoo-*yeah*." Color rushed into her face matching the velocity of the heat washing through his body. "I said that out loud, didn't I?"

He grinned. "Yes, ma'am."

Closing her eyes, she groaned, "Go look out the window and count cars or something." She re-opened her eyes and waved him away. "I can't think when you..."

"When I what?" He leaned closer, wanting to hear her finish.

She sighed. "When you're near. Now...go look out the window and take your focus with you."

"Yes, ma'am," he repeated, a grin still on his face as he did as she bid and stood in front of her floor-to-ceiling window. The sun was starting to set, but the traffic remained busy as day transitioned to night over the city. Way up here, the sounds were faint. The frantic pace was below, and for the first time in a long time, he took a good look at the city.

The mix of ethnicities was still there. The hard workers were still there. So were the predators and the police trying to get them off the streets. None of that was new. The city hadn't changed, it had just updated, with an even stronger resilience. His father had loved that about the city. Archer too, but he truthfully missed his boat. Missed the ocean. Missed his little piece of heaven on the shore and looked forward to leaving this city behind to relax away from the crowds.

But not away from Sandy.

He listened to her humming to herself as she clacked on her keyboard. No, he wasn't leaving until they sat down and drafted a plan to see each other...

The hair on the back of his neck stood up.

He stilled, and glanced across the street, but with the setting sun glaring right in the area where there was no building to block it, Archer couldn't see a damn thing. Christ, someone could be pointing a tank at him and he wouldn't see it.

They needed to leave. Now. Since he had no idea who was watching them or how, he wasn't about to make it easy for the bastards to follow them back to their Brooklyn safe house. He pulled out his phone and sent a text alert to Bella, informing her they needed a hot extraction—EXFIL—two blocks south.

"You about ready?" he asked calmly, making sure to keep his body in line with hers to block any projectiles.

"Yep," she said. "Just powering down."

Archer turned to face her. "Good. Lets' go," he said, ushering her into the hall.

"What's wrong?" She stepped in front of him to place a hand on his chest to stop him. "What's going on?"

CHAPTER TEN

"We're being watched. We need to get out now," Archer muttered, grabbing her hand as he walked with her down the hall, his gaze peeled for any sudden movements.

The reception area was clear. As a matter of fact, it was too clear. He punched the button for the elevators, noting one appeared to be stuck three floors down and the other on the fifth floor.

Shit.

He reached down and yanked his gun from his ankle holster then stood. "Tell me there's another set of stairs…" He wasn't about to use the closest one.

"Yes. This way." Sandy rushed toward her office and halfway there she turned right and pointed to an exit sign at the end of that hall.

They ran to it and Archer entered first, checking up then down, before motioning for her to follow. They made it down eight flights and were moving past the sixth floor door when it jerked opened, knocking Sandy backward toward the wall.

Unable to shoot because she was too close, Archer launched himself at the man dressed in black tactical gear and the momentum propelled them into the hall, where they smashed into two more men wearing the same gear. The impact knocked two of three weapons away, but not his.

With Sandy no longer near the men, Archer shot the guy closest to him, grabbed the man's falling weapon and emptied it into the two remaining men struggling to get back on their feet.

Sandy rushed in. "Archer, are you okay?"

Jesus...

"Yes, but I don't want you running into the gunfire," he muttered, grabbing her arm. "Let's go."

"No...wait" She yanked free. "Remove their masks," she said, fishing her phone from her purse, then grimaced as she took their photos. "Okay."

He swiped one of the unused handguns off the floor and re-checked the stairwell before motioning for her to enter.

"Wait." She halted. "I should take one of their guns, too."

He sucked in a breath. "No...let's just keep moving," he growled, resisting the urge to rub his shoulder. Damn thing ached like a son-of-a-bitch. Charging into those assholes aggravated his injury. But he didn't care. He just wanted to get her the hell out of there.

Thank Christ, she listened and headed down the stairs. "Should I call security?" she asked on their descent. "I'm sure they heard that gunfire."

"No. Right now, I don't trust anyone but *you* in this place." With both of his arms outstretched, weapons gripped in each hand, Archer kept his body in front of hers as they made their way to the bottom floor. Once there, he checked outside, surprised to find the area clear.

What the hell?

Holstering his gun, he shoved the procured one in his waistband under his shirt and pulled her from the building. This damn mission made less and less sense. Sliding his arm around Sandy's waist, Archer gripped her hip to keep her close as they joined the workforce crowd gathered at the end of the block, eager to make their way home. He could relate. Scanning the area, he saw nothing amiss, but felt too vulnerable...too out in the open. He needed to get Sandy somewhere safe.

Four minutes later, they made it the two blocks to EXFIL, without incident, where Bella pulled up to the curb and they hoped into...Sandy's SUV?

"Why do you have Sandy's vehicle?" he asked, after they got settled into the back seat.

Bella met his gaze in the rearview mirror. "TJ needs to access Jimmy's computer at the bank, so Matteo took him."

Sandy stiffened. "Who's watching the prisoners?"

He could see a smile spread across Bella's face, as she merged into traffic. "Don't worry about them, they're still tied up, locked up...and unconscious."

"What'd you get out of them?" he asked, knowing she was the reason they were unconscious.

The woman stopped at a light and turned to him. "They're lackeys. Compartmentalized lackeys. Jimmy's usefulness is his access to the bank. That's why TJ and Matteo are there, to see if they can trace what they're using him for, and if we're lucky, *who* is doing the using. And hoodie-dude is a thug.

Darnel DeJesus Jackson is a hired strong-arm with a long history of gang violence, petty theft, aggravated assault...the list goes on and on. Mental capacity beyond that is nil."

And poor Stan had gotten in his path. He could've just pushed him out of the way but instead, the bastard stabbed him.

"So..." The woman glanced at them in the rearview mirror again. "You couldn't invite me to kill bad guys with you?"

He blew out a breath. Matteo had his hands full with her. Then again, that man always did love a challenge. Archer supposed the couple was evenly matched, although, he had the feeling his friend deserved a medal for patience.

"We didn't invite the bad guys, either," Sandy said. "Next time—"

"Next time?" He reeled back. *Fuck...no.* "There's not going to be a next time," he growled, yanking his phone out of his pocket to place a call to Silas. "Branson? You've got a goddamn mole in your New York DHS office." He went on to explain the latest incident. "You may want to take care of the mess on the sixth floor, too. And make them clean house. Find this mole. Sandy won't be back until it's spotless." While he had the man on the line, he brought him up to speed about the audio match, and the two prisoners and what they'd discovered about the men so far.

He intended to get more out of them and would've, if he hadn't been busy being involved in a shootout at fucking Homeland.

A warm hand covered his clenched fist, and he blinked before turning to meet Sandy's gaze. There he found more warmth, and a beautiful smile that mouthed the words "thank you."

He entwined his fingers with her trembling ones and squeezed. She didn't need to thank him. It was his pleasure to watch over her, he just hated that there was a need for it.

After promising to keep Silas informed, Archer hung up and rode the rest of the way back to Brooklyn with his hand still entwined with Sandy's. He didn't want to let her go. He needed the connection. She grounded him. Calmed him. And he liked to think he did the same for her, because she was no longer shaking.

There were times her touch fogged his brain and times, like now, when he saw things clearly. It was crazy. And a godsend because when Bella drove through the abandoned warehouse to the garage area, the hairs on the back of his neck stood up again.

"Stop," he ordered, releasing Sandy's hand.

"What is it?" she asked.

He shook his head. "Stay here," he told her before exiting the vehicle.

Bella got out and glanced around, as well. "Your Spidey senses going off, too?"

"Yeah, something's off." To look at the area, though, it appeared fine. He'd learned plenty of times across the pond that meant shit. He possessed a handheld monitor with live feed from inside the base, but it wouldn't detect trip wires. "Do you have any equipment with you?" The other SUV had the surveillance kit.

Bella produced a handheld laser and swept the area, paying close attention to the door.

He muttered a curse when it flagged a trip wire at the base, and it wasn't one of TJ's, because they hadn't set any up at this location. A heavy sense of dread filled his chest. He pulled out the monitor and flicked through the rooms to see what awaited them if they tried to enter.

Sandy got out of the SUV, and Bella walked over to view it with him. One room at a time, they studied the monitor, looking for signs of intruders or bombs. Archer's heart dropped into his gut when he got to the prisoners' cells and found them both naked...and dead. Throats cut.

Fuck.

Sandy inhaled and covered her mouth with her hand.

Bella muttered an oath in Italian. "It wasn't me," she said. "We stripped them in case they were wearing trackers or wires, but they were alive—unconscious, but *alive*—when I left." She cursed again. He wasn't sure if it was because they were dead or because she hadn't been the one to do it.

"Thank God TJ and Matteo weren't here," Sandy muttered.

Bella shook her head. "This would never have happened if they were."

Good point.

"Someone is watching. They waited for us to all leave," he said, glancing around, frustrated as shit at not having the upper hand.

The sudden clicking sound, followed by a beeping that grew louder and louder, sent him into action.

"Get in the SUV," he ordered. "We have to go. Now!"

He practically pushed Sandy inside and got in next to her, closing the door before he covered her with his body as Bella jumped back into the driver's seat and fishtailed them backward out of the garage area. Then she slammed it in drive and punched it as a rumbling sounded beneath the earth, followed by an explosion that rocked the ground, and the whole warehouse swayed.

Son-of-a-bitch. Someone had definitely been watching and set off the bomb when they realized he and the others weren't going to go inside.

Steel beams creaked with a sickening sound, and Bella swerved around pieces of ceiling that began to fall as she raced for the opening in the busted bay door. They passed through as another explosion brought the rest of the dilapidated building down.

"Keep driving," he told Bella even though they were clear.

She slowed down and zigzagged through Brooklyn, while answering her phone. "I'm fine," she reassured—her husband, no doubt. "Did TJ get what he needed? Good."

"You okay?" he asked Sandy, slowly moving off her to help her sit up when he felt she was no longer threatened.

Inhaling, she met his gaze and nodded. "Yeah. You?"

115

He blew out a breath and nodded too, lifting a hand to push the hair from her face that he'd knocked loose from her bun. "I'm good."

"I'm going to put you on speaker," Bella said. "Archer and Sandy are with me."

"What the hell just happened?" Matteo's voice echoed through the SUV.

Sandy nodded. "How did they know our location?"

"And get past my security?" TJ asked.

Archer clenched his teeth and his jaw cracked. "I'm not sure, but I'm going to find out."

"I have a theory on how they knew where we were," Bella said, then continued when Archer nodded, "It was the prisoners."

Sandy frowned. "But I thought you said you stripped them in case they were being tracked."

"We did," Bella replied. "But we never searched under their skin."

Archer raised a brow. "You think they were injected?"

"Cool." TJ's intrigued tone sounded through the speaker.

Bella nodded. "Yes. It's the only way. The only thing that makes sense, because I swept their clothes before I burned them, and they were clean."

Archer made a mental note to check the feed when they re-grouped. TJ always backed up his feed, so they would be able to zoom in on the prisoner's forearms to look for a mark left by the tiny incision required. The chance of it still being visible, though, was a different story. The procedure would've had to have been recent.

He intended to check the feed to see exactly who the hell had broken into the place. Whoever they were, they had to be as good at hacking as TJ. "We need to regroup," he said. "Since we're not sure if our communications are compromised, let's follow Protocol 9."

"Roger that," Matteo said. "I'll call Knight to send in a cleanup team."

Good. He didn't want anyone to get their hands on things they shouldn't. "See you at the rendezvous."

"Roger that," Matteo said again, then the line went dead.

Bella shoved her phone back in her pocket and glanced at him in the rearview. "We need to ditch this vehicle."

"Agreed." He nodded.

Sandy stiffened. "By ditch, you mean park it somewhere safe, right?"

Bella met his gaze again. He nodded. "For now."

"Okay, then can I suggest near my apartment?" She looked hopefully at him. "Because my laptop is toast, and I need access to my backup files on my desktop."

Shit.

"It's the only place it's backed up, Archer," she said, covering his hand with hers, her gaze intense. Serious. "I need it. Not just for this case, but for others."

He blew out a breath. "Fine. Let's go rescue your hard drive."

If there wasn't time to take the computer apart and remove the hard drive, then they'd just take the whole tower.

But when they pulled onto her street fifteen minutes later, lights flashed as an ambulance and two police cars blocked the wraparound entrance.

Sandy stiffened and scooted closer to peer out his window. "What do you think is going on?"

"Looks like a body," Bella said, slowing down to a crawl.

Sandy sucked in a breath. "Oh my God, Archer. I think that's Rodrigo..."

It was. He'd gotten a good look as they drove past. His insides fisted, then twisted as a tear fell down Sandy's cheek. He slid his arm around her shoulders and hugged her to him. There wasn't anything he could say so he didn't.

"What do you want me to do?" Bella asked, meeting his gaze in the mirror.

Sandy stiffened then drew out of his arms. "What do you mean?" She frowned at Bella. "You have to stop. We need to get my computer."

Archer reached for her hand. "Not right now."

"But we have to—"

"I know," he said gently, cutting her off. "And we will. But not now. We need the proper equipment."

She frowned. "For what?"

"For disabling tripwires," Bella said. "There's a better than a hundred percent chance your place is rigged."

He felt Sandy inhale, and her eyes were wide when they met his and blinked. He nodded. "We'll get it. We just need to prepare."

"Trust me." Bella smiled at her in the mirror. "With the proper accessories, I can get in without tripping anything. Then disable, dismantle, and leave undetected.

He nodded. "It's time we operate a step ahead." Because he sure-as-hell was tired of working two fucking steps behind.

"Okay." Sandy sighed and leaned into him. "I don't want anyone else to get hurt."

"Hey," he said, slipping his arm around her shoulder again. "Whatever happened to Rodrigo was not on you or me. It's on the bastards who did it."

Or Rodrigo himself, if he was part of the group they were after.

She nodded, but more tears spilled down her face. His insides twisted again. He kissed her head and pulled her in closer. The woman's compassion sucked him in, but he needed to keep his focus sharp.

As Bella turned the corner, he glanced at the scene, seeing it for what it really was, while he held Sandy close.

If he hadn't been sure before, he was damn certain now.

That was a warning.

Whoever this was—whoever was doing this shit—they knew where Sandy worked. Knew where she lived. Knew where he'd hidden her. And now all three were compromised.

He needed to get her somewhere safe. Somewhere off the grid.

Somewhere off the Atlantic coast.

***

After parking her vehicle in a nice neighborhood—she'd insisted, because she was still paying on it, dammit—Sandy walked with Archer a few blocks to a nearby all-night food store where Bella met them with their new, temporary ride. A black SUV.

"Don't worry, I'll return it when we come back for your computer," Bella assured her with a grin.

Sandy felt better knowing the owner wouldn't be put out for long. It was one thing to interfere in the lives of criminals and those who intend to do harm, but causing chaos for the innocent didn't sit right with her at all.

She nodded and got in next to Archer, only this time, she didn't scurry over seats. She got in on her own side. The only downfall was not sitting close to him. Even just the slight touch of their knees or brush of their arms went a long way to calming her insides.

When Bella took the exit for the Holland Tunnel, Sandy glanced over at the silent SEAL sitting next to her. "We're going to New Jersey?"

"Yes." He nodded. "I want you out of the city. Once you have your computer, or your hard drive from it, you can just as easily work from my place as you can from another New York safe house."

Her heart leapt and the force reeled her back slightly. "Your place?"

"Yes," he said again. "I know you'll be safe there."

She wasn't as sure. "Surely these people know who you are, since you've been around me at work. Won't they know where you live as well?"

A sexy, sure smile pulled his dimples to life, and tripped her pulse. "No. I purchased my house and my boat through a silent corporation, not my name. I've seen too many things. Done too many things, to ever take that chance."

"Oh." She sighed, feeling oddly better when she probably should be alarmed. "So, are we going to your house or your boat?"

He cocked his head and narrowed his eyes for a moment. "I was originally thinking the boat, but the house might be better tonight."

"Plus, you'll be closer to the nest," Bella said, meeting their gaze in the rearview mirror.

Sandy frowned, splitting her attention between them. "Nest?"

"Knight headquarters in AC," the woman said, as if that made things clear.

It didn't.

"What is the night headquarters?" she asked. "Do you have a different one for during the day?"

"No. Not, n-i-g-h-t." Archer smiled. "K-n-i-g-h-t, as in Knight Agency. Bella's boss."

She blinked at Archer. "Oh, yeah…that's right. You did mention they all worked for the Knight Agency."

Bella grinned. "We're on loan."

Sandy rubbed her temples. It'd been another long day. Her mind was all jumbled. "So the Knight Agency has a headquarters in Atlantic City?"

"Yes," Archer said. "Jameson Knight is an old SEAL buddy of mine. He has several agencies up and down the East Coast. Bella and Matteo run the AC satellite office."

The name Jameson Knight sounded vaguely familiar to her, though. Probably through work. She stared at Bella. "And you refer to your AC office as 'the nest.'"

"Exactly." Their chauffer nodded. "After I drop you two off, I'm going there to meet up with Matteo, grab our gear, and head back to Queens to disable whatever surprises are in your apartment and secure your hard drive."

Her heart rocked. "You're going back tonight?"

"Yep." Bella nodded.

"The sooner the better," Archer said, placing his hand on hers. "Don't worry. They'll make sure your neighbors are safe."

She blew out a long breath. "And I'll feel better knowing they are when they're done."

"I'll be sure to shoot Archer a text afterward," Bella said, slowing down to pull into a driveway.

Sandy glanced at the dashboard clock and was shocked to realize they'd been driving for over two hours.

"Good." He nodded, opening the door. "Tomorrow, we'll meet up, regroup, and go on the offensive."

"Roger that," Bella said. "Have a good night."

Before she could reply, Archer opened her door and helped her out. She managed to wave as Bella backed out of the driveway, then she turned to stare at a cute, quaint little cottage with the Atlantic Ocean as a backyard.

He opened the door, turned on the lights, and ushered her inside. The open-concept surprised her, and so did the warm, comfortable décor, but it was the view that beckoned. She walked straight to the back to look out the sliding doors.

"Go on out." He unlocked the door and tugged it open.

Sandy eagerly stepped onto the deck, closed her eyes, and inhaled the ocean air. Perfect. Almost. She reached up, removed the elastic from her hair, and shook it out, enjoying the feel of the wind blowing through it.

Now it was perfect.

Opening her eyes, she exhaled and gazed out over the ocean. The moon shined brightly overhead, and the sound of waves crashing onto the shore immediately calmed her mind.

If this was her piece of heaven, she'd never leave.

"It's something, isn't it?" he asked quietly from behind her.

She could feel him standing close and it only added to the contentment washing over her. "Absolutely. I envy you this." She turned to face him, fascinated at how the glow from the moon illuminated the silver streaks in his hair and turned the gray of his eyes a gorgeous, silver hue.

"My dad bought it," he said, and went on to mention his fun childhood, and explained how he'd purchased the house from his mother and fixed it up to his father's standards. "And I can't believe I just told you all that," he said, using a finger to brush a strand of hair behind her ear where his finger lingered.

She reached up to touch the wrist of that hand. "I can."

He said her name on a sucked in breath and slowly lowered his mouth to hers, kissing one corner of her mouth, then the other, then slid full on to sweetly, thoroughly kiss the strength from her legs. Sandy moaned, and clutched his shoulders, loving the feel of his muscles bunching under her touch, while his tongue made slow, drugging sweeps of her mouth, over and over in a sweet assault on her senses.

When they finally broke for air, she realized he'd switched them around and maneuvered them so he was standing on the deck with his back to the ocean, and she was standing just inside the door.

"You are far too special for me to take that kiss where it was headed," he murmured, brushing her cheek with his thumb before releasing her to grab the handle on the door. "Explore the house. Make yourself at home. Take whichever room you want. Take a shower, bake cookies, have a beer." He smiled. "Do whatever you want. I'm going to hang out here for a bit and contemplate the meaning of life and possibly cool off in the ocean."

She inhaled. "You can't. The water temperature is too cold."

It was only April.

He chuckled. "Not for my affliction. Trust me." And with one, last, pained look at her lips, he closed the door and turned away.

Well...darn.

She drew in several deep breaths and steadied her erratic heartbeats. That was the sweetest, single most honest thing anyone had ever said to or done for her, and Sandy had the ache in her chest to prove it.

Out of respect for *his* respect for her...she forced herself to walk away from the door and explore his house as per his request.

The kitchen was a dream kitchen, plain and simple. New appliances. Big stove. Big sink. Attractive island/snack bar facing an open living room. A nice sized dining room table sat in front of the door she was staying away from, and the master bedroom and guest bedroom were cozy and inviting, but the bathroom was the room she hesitated to leave. There was a gorgeous soaking tub—she estimated was big enough for them both to fit at the same time—and a large, walk-in shower that made her whole-body tingle just imagining water running down the lean, muscular body of the man outside.

Since he was obviously trying not to think about those decadent things, Sandy figured she shouldn't either. Walking into his kitchen, she thought perhaps she should whip them up something quick for a late supper. It'd been awhile since they'd had any food. The last thing they ate was...hot dogs from Rodrigo.

Her stomach clenched tightly. And what really sucked, was she had no idea if it was okay to grieve the young man...or if he had been involved with whatever the hell was going on. He certainly had no reason to be at her apartment in Queens. Especially since she'd just seen him less than two hours earlier in front of DHS.

Where someone was attempting to shoot her...

She slumped against the kitchen counter and stared at her feet.

She'd eaten from his cart outside the World Bank, then the next morning someone tried to barbeque her. She had another hot dog from him today, and a half hour later, someone tried to shoot her. Damn. She sighed and the sound echoed around her in the quiet house. He definitely had something to do with the mess going on.

But was his involvement voluntary or unknowingly?

She was determined to figure that out.

The sound of the sliding door opening disappeared under the roar the waves made hitting the beach outside. Archer stepped inside and closed the door, muffling the sweet symphony of the shore. His clothes were dry, so no swimming took place, she was happy to note.

"How was your...contemplation?" she asked, straightening from the counter.

He stared at her from across the space of two rooms, yet it felt like they were mere inches apart. "Too long."

"Long?" She glanced at the clock on the microwave and chuckled. "You've only been outside nine minutes."

"True." He left his stance by the door and strode straight to her, his gait determined and sure, his gaze deliciously dark, with a heat that set her temperature to slow burn. "Nine minutes I could've spent in here with you."

CHAPTER ELEVEN

Sandy's heart rocked, and she couldn't breathe. Couldn't think. As always, Archer's presence was all consuming, but with his attention, his focus fully on her, she felt...everything and all at once. The strong, sexy SEAL was saying things she'd secretly longed to hear for years. Awareness tumbled down her body, and she leaned against the counter again for support, while her mind tried to compute what her eyes were seeing.

He stopped in front of her and palmed the cabinet behind her head. Sandy's attempt to suck in some air ended up clogging her throat.

Was this really happening?

Or was he going to back off again? They seemed to be involved in a pull and push dance the past few days. But was Archer actually coming on to her this time?

It'd happened countless times in her dreams. Right now, though, Sandy couldn't tell fantasy from reality.

"It's no use." He lifted a finger to trace a path from her ear to her jaw, his gaze focused on the movement. "I was trying not to cross that *family off-limits* line, but you and I both know we charged right over it on that street corner near the bank."

With her voice still stuck in her clogged throat, she nodded. What an amazing charge it had been, too. The hottest kiss of her life.

"So…now we have a problem. No matter how many scenarios I run through my head, and trust me, I've run many," he said, voice low and so damn sexy she shook. "We have a big problem."

The only problem she analyzed was the amount of clothes separating their bodies from a release she knew they both needed. Fighting this chemistry was no longer an option for her.

She cleared her throat and held his gaze. "What problem? Maybe I can help."

"Help?" His finger skimmed her lower lip, sending jolts of heat straight to all her good parts. "Can you stop looking at me like you want me inside you?"

She inhaled and slowly shook her head, causing his finger to brush more of her lip. "No."

His eyes darkened on that one and jaw clenched tight. "No?"

"Not when you touch me," she replied. "Or look at me like you want to inhale me."

He did inhale—not her—but air, then removed his touch and moved until the kitchen island separated them. "Then we definitely have a problem, Sandy, because I can't seem to keep my damn hands off you. And I want to be in you. I want to taste you, make you mine…make you scream my name while I come inside you."

Swift and hot, desire rushed through her veins with a velocity that propelled her forward. His words and rough tone—raw with the same fierce need trembling through her—stole the strength from her legs. She reached for the island and gripped tight. "What if I wanted all those things, too?"

Muttering a curse, he white-knuckled the counter across from her, but remained silent. Just held her gaze.

Sandy decided to go a little further. Get a little brazen. "So why don't you?"

Archer closed his eyes and sucked in a breath. "You're going to be the death of me."

"Ditto," she muttered, her body hot and shaky.

Opening his eyes, Archer stared at her, gaze full of hunger, yet clouded with restraint. "I want you, Sandy. Very much. But…your son is a SEAL."

She blinked.

That's what this is about?

Her attraction for Archer back then had been unexpected, but she'd managed to squash it down. She knew the score. Knew the *family off-limits* code. But it no longer applied, and she was done putting her needs second.

"I know." She nodded. "And I think I've been a pretty good mom. When my husband died, I buried my needs and my wants. I put my child first. I was his mother and his father. He was my world. *Still* is…but he's living his own life now, and it's time I started to live mine. Besides, Brian is no longer under your command."

Archer lifted his chin. "But *you* are."

"True." She sighed. He was her boss. "So…I guess that means I have to bury my wants and needs again."

He blew out a breath and nodded. "As will I. But only until the job is done, Sandy."

She smiled, despite the disappointment swirling inside. "Okay." She liked the promise in his tone and gleam in his eyes. It would be worth the wait. And she certainly didn't want to compromise his beliefs or command.

He nodded again, then pivoted on his heel and marched out of the house and onto his back deck again. A second later, the sliding door clicked into place, leaving her alone with her unsatisfied desire and raging disappointment.

She'd get over it. She was used to putting herself second.

But only until the job is done...

A thrilled rippled down her body, stoking a few of desire's lingering embers. Archer's words—his promise—remained in her head. The determination that had glinted in his gaze left her in no doubt that the man would make good on that promise. And when he did...it would be *happy birthday* to her.

The door slid open, Archer stepped back inside and closed it, before setting the alarm by the door. Then he turned to face her.

"If we give into this chemistry..." he said, "...will it affect your work?"

She swallowed past her suddenly dry throat and stared at the man hovering by the door. The very fact he'd asked that question signaled he'd changed his mind about waiting. "Yes." She nodded, watching his brow furrow. "But in a good way."

"Oh?" He lifted that brow.

"I'll have clarity of mind," she replied, and decided to lay it all out. "It won't be so darn fogged with unsatisfied need for you."

He blinked. "Unsatisfied need? For me?"

"Yes." She frowned. "Why is that so hard to believe?"

He shook his head. "Damn, Sandy…you're way too classy for my sorry ass."

She held back a grin. "Take that back, Malone," she said, tipping her head. "I'm from Queens. I'm not classy. I'm sassy."

"That, too." A smile tugged at his very kissable lips. "You're also smart and beautiful and could have anyone you want. Not an old bonefrog bum like me."

"I happen to like that part of you. A lot." She held his gaze, letting him see in hers just how much she was attracted to him. "You're strong. Loyal. Brash. You've seen the best and the worst humanity has to offer and still you put your life on the line for people. Combine all that with the silver at your temples…and you take my breath away, Archer."

His gaze darkened to a delicious chrome hue that made her tremble.

"And I look forward to when we can act on this chemistry between us. Whether it's now…or in the future," she told him. "I know it'll be worth the wait."

She could be wrong, but she thought she heard him growl before he strode from the sliding door toward her again, his gaze and gait returning to that determination from earlier, spiking her already thundering pulse.

"I agree," he said, stopping in front of her to brush her lower lip with his thumb. "But I don't want to wait."

Her heart dipped to her belly then returned to her chest, racing like mad. He was back to saying the things she'd longed to hear. "You don't?"

Once again, they were engaged in the "pull" part of their dance.

Her favorite part.

"No, I don't want to wait." He shook his head and ran his hands lightly down her arms and back up. "I'm done waiting, Sandy. I want you. Right here. Right now. To hell with everything else."

She lifted a hand to palm his solid chest while her other gripped his hip. "Good, because I want you and your *bone*frog."

He chuckled and set his forehead to hers. "I just don't want you to get hurt."

"Why? Is it that big?" she teased.

He choked out a laugh. "I didn't mean that."

"I know." She smiled. "And I appreciate it. And you." She slipped her hands under his shirt and brushed his hot flesh all the way to his pecs, thrilled at how his big, hard body quivered under her touch. "What about you? What do you want?" She grazed a fingernail over one of his nipples and was rewarded with a hiss of breath.

"More of that." He pressed into her. "I love the feel of your hands on my body."

"Roger that."

He grinned, his gaze heated and direct. "I think it's way past time I put mine on yours," he murmured, skimming a palm down the front of her, brushing lightly over her breast. His wicked thumb lingered on her peak, brushing it back and forth, detonating brain cell after brain cell.

Heat rushed between her legs, and she arched into his touch. "Yes. Past time…"

In a blink of an eye, he had her pressed against the wall between the sliding glass door and kitchen, with his strong, rock-hard body. He shoved his hands in her hair and stared into her eyes. "Are you sure about this, Sandy? If you have any reservations tell me now, because once we start, it'll be difficult to stop. I've wanted you for far too long."

"I'm beyond sure, Archer," she muttered, and rocked against him to prove it.

The last of his restraint disappeared from his gaze, leaving nothing but raw, fierce need. "Then it's time I made you call my name." He dipped down to drag his mouth up her throat. "Loud, soft, doesn't matter," he murmured against her skin, "Because I aim to hear it *all* fall from your lips tonight." Drawing back, he shoved a hand in his pocket before slapping several condoms on the nearby table. "*Multiple*…times."

She inhaled, and he captured her open mouth, kissing her without restraint, his hunger for her a lot stronger than she'd imagined. Sandy moaned, and ran her hands around his back to pull him in closer.

As fierce, hot, and demanding as the man, his kiss made her want to give more, to feel more, to be more. Deep and long, thorough and complete, it rocked her world and turned it upside down in the best way. Sandy's body throbbed with a need she never knew she'd possessed. Thankfully, this hot, capable, gorgeous man no longer regarded her as the mother of one of his SEALs.

Gone was his self-discipline, his restraint. Archer kissed away her sanity, and her ability to stand. Over and over, he devoured her strength, his tongue stroking hers, his hands caressing her body, bringing it to life in a blaze of heat.

When they came up for air, she stared at him, trying to grasp onto a coherent thought, but only need for the man persisted in her head.

Dragging in air, he cracked a sexy grin and it snagged her heart. Damn, he looked delectable, with his shirt...*gone*? Geeze...when had she done that? He made her nuts. So did the dusting of hair across his chest her fingers were still stroking. The sight of the ridges in his abs did funny things to her breathing, which wasn't steady by any means. Neither was her equilibrium, because somehow, she'd managed to unbuckle the top of his jeans without realizing it, too.

Yeah. She was off-kilter and out of her league and loving every damn second. She felt carefree, wild, unhindered. He pushed her boundaries, took her out of herself.

She knew it. She *knew* he would. And God, wouldn't it be great if she was doing the same to him?

Sandy set her forehead against his chin. "That was...wow...I've been missing out."

"So have I." He slipped a hand under her shirt to stroke her above the curve of her hip, and goosebumps shot down her side. "But we're not going to miss out anymore."

She stood there trembling, as he used both hands to grab the neck of the T-shirt he'd bought earlier that day and ripped it off her body.

It was the sexiest damn thing she'd ever experienced, although the raw need deepening his gaze to a smoky shade of gray made all her good parts pulse.

"Damn, Sandy…"

Spurred on by his desire, she reached behind her and unhooked her bra, hoping he wasn't turned off by the fact gravity had unfriended her since she'd turned forty last month. Letting her bra fall to the floor, she watched mesmerized as his gaze darkened further at the sight of her bared breasts.

"You're so perfect."

Perfect?

He was perfect. Not an ounce of fat on his hard, muscular torso, with definition and ridges making her mouth water.

He reached out and cupped her breasts, seeming not to notice or care that they weren't so perky. "Damn perfect," he murmured, dipping down to draw a nipple into his mouth and tease with his tongue.

"Archer," she gasped, grasping his upper arms, loving the feel of his muscles rippling under her fingers.

Switching to her other breast, he caught the tip between his teeth and tugged while his hands slid down her body and unhooked her pants.

Sandy gasped again.

He released her nipple to kiss and nip his way down her body as he pushed her jeans and panties to her feet. "So damn perfect," he murmured, glancing up at her nakedness. He caressed every inch of her as he rose to his feet, except where she needed it most.

He had her hot and trembling and needing more.

Needing everything.

"Hold on to me," he ordered before he gripped her hips and twisted them around to set her on the dining room table. His gaze darkened as her curves bounced, and a second later, her shoes and the rest of her clothes were on the floor. A sexy sound rumbled in his throat. "Gorgeous." He glided his hands up her inner thighs, and his fingers brushed her center, finally touching the part that ached for him the most.

"Archer." His name ripped from her throat again, this time in a voice full of hunger and need, as she clutched at his arms and rocked into his touch.

He let out a rough groan. "So wet..." His lips were hot and demanding as he captured her mouth in a fierce, hungry kiss while he stroked her again and again.

She moaned and ran her hands down his chest and abs, reveling at the feel of his body quivering under her touch. Using that hot, hard body, he pressed her down until her back hit the table. Damn, he felt so good. Solid. Hard. Flesh brushing flesh. Then he drew back, and removed his finger, and she was about to protest when he gently grasped her ankles and set her legs over his shoulders.

His inhale cooled the air around her thighs, and she watched him clench his jaw, his expression caught somewhere between pleasure and pain. And before she could blink, he leaned in and put his mouth on her, stroking her with his tongue.

She cried out and jumped. It'd been *so* long...decades since she'd had oral sex.

"Easy," he murmured, placing a hand on her belly to hold her steady. "I got you."

And he did, but good. The incredible man was thorough and commanding—and on a

mission—because he added a finger, sliding it inside her as he flicked his tongue over her aching center.

Sandy's gasp turned into a moan, and both echoed around them. This seemed to spur him on. He upped his pace, and she clutched the edges of the table and held tight, while he continued to take her on a journey of pure pleasure. It felt so good...

She didn't remember it feeling this good. Unable to keep still, she rocked against him while teetering on that warm, blissful edge.

"Archer," she whispered. "I need..."

Coherent thoughts were tough to hold onto with the strong, giving, virile man in charge of her body.

He glanced at her, gaze delectably dark with a fierce hunger and determination that was nearly her undoing. "I've got you," he repeated before sucking her gently into his mouth.

That was it. She was done.

All those years of wanting Archer and wondering what it would be like to be with him came to fruition at that very moment. Sandy burst, and he used his expertise to prolong her pleasure as he held her hips and gently brought her down from that warm deliciousness.

When her mind cleared and vision returned, she let out a sigh and met his gaze. Her heart knocked into her ribs. His eyes—damn, they smoldered with pure male satisfaction. Heat immediately flickered through her satiated body.

Seriously? How could he have her ready with a single glance?

"What just happened?"

Releasing her, he straightened, and a sexy, deliciously possessive grin claimed his lips. "I made you mine."

A thrill shot through her at crazy speed. She knew he respected her and that her body was hers to do as she pleased. But his words exhilarated her too. She was also aware that his words really meant she was making *him* hers. That he needed to brand her—to stand out—to guarantee she'd remember *him* and how he made her feel.

As if she'd ever forget...

Holding her gaze, he pulled his zipper down and shucked the rest of his clothes, and when he straightened, she sat up to run a hand over his chest. His body vibrated with a tension she felt clear to her core. He grabbed a condom from the pile he'd set on the table earlier, and needing to have him inside her, she reached down to help roll the condom over the length of him.

And there was plenty of length. *Thick* length. Her insides pulsed in anticipation of what was to come.

He muttered a curse, breathing heavy, a sheen of sweat breaking out across his brow. "Killing me."

Feeling inspired and empowered, she smiled and leaned in to flick her tongue over his nipple. He cursed, grabbed her hips, and positioning his tip at her center, he slowly pushed inside.

Her cry of pleasure mingled with his, as he shoved all the way in.

The man filled her so completely, she could barely catch her breath. It was amazing.

"You okay?" He stared, concern replacing some of the heat.

"Yes…don't stop." And to prove she meant it, Sandy wrapped her legs around him and locked her ankles behind his well-formed ass.

This drew him in even farther, and their sounds of approval blended around them.

"Damn, Sandy," he dragged in air, "you feel so damn good."

His gaze was deliciously dark—almost black—as he began to move. Clutching his shoulders, she rocked into him, moaning at the sensual feel of their bodies connecting. Over and over, he plunged in and withdrew nearly all the way out, holding her hips for his slow, exquisite thrusts.

There was no doubt now, he was in control. His grip prevented her from upping the pace. He was in command, and heaven help her, she loved it.

And if his vigilant, purposeful thrusts weren't enough to drive her out of her ever-loving mind, he tested her own control when he bent down to capture a nipple in his mouth. She cried out, her eyes rolling in the back of her head as he made his way to the other. The incredible, mindless pleasure took her right up to that blissful edge again.

"Archer." She tightened her grip on his shoulders.

"I know," he said, voice rough as he kissed her neck and continued to stroke her with those fierce thrusts. "Me, too."

Knowing this strong, incredible, retired SEAL commander was just as lost in the mindless pleasure was all it took to propel her over the edge along with the man who'd so often visited her dreams. But Sandy discovered those dreams were nothing compared to the real SEAL as she called out his name while he came inside her.

Reality was so much better…so much more, she thought, as she clung to his hot, hard, magnificent body, their shared release shaking through them with a consuming heat.

***

Last night, Archer had discovered heaven *did* exist on earth. He'd found it in the arms of the beauty curled up against him, all warm and soft and curvy. He carefully stretched out in his bed, early morning sunlight streaking through the shades, casting bright lines across the comforter covering their naked bodies.

A first for him—sharing his bed with a woman. Even during his relationship with Helen it hadn't happened. He'd shared her condo until she'd had the abortion. After that, he'd moved back on base and closed part of himself off, only enjoying a hookup now and then. It was always time spent at the woman's place. Never his rental, and definitely never in his bed. He refused to share his personal space or give anyone the opportunity to stake a claim on him—to forge that kind of connection ever again.

Until Sandy.

Bending his head toward hers resting on his pillow, he inhaled. She smelled like his bodywash from their shared shower last night, but mixed with the delectable, sweet scent of Sandy. It was imprinted in his sheets...and his mind. So was the feel and taste of her. A smile tugged his lips while heat skittered through his body.

Yesterday, before cleaning the table—at Sandy's insistence—and showering—at his insistence—they'd tested the integrity of the cushion on the overstuffed armchair, deeming it worthy. He especially liked the way the she rode him when he was buried balls deep inside her sweet curves, her luscious breasts bouncing close to his face while she bucked wildly the instant he brushed his thumb over her center. Yeah, he really liked that part. She'd made the sexiest damn sounds he'd ever heard.

Ah, hell.

He let out a slow breath. He was rock-hard again. How was it possible?

He should be dead.

Apparently, his raging hard-on was testament to the fact he couldn't seem to get enough of the woman. That was why, after their shower, he'd passed by the guest room she was supposed to use and carried her straight into his room.

Sandy belonged with him.

In his space.

In his bed...at least during her time spent in New Jersey.

The woman made him want things. Made him feel things. Made him *not* feel things—like the ache in his shoulder. He'd barely noticed the pain the whole time he'd been concentrating on her.

"Mmm..." She stirred next to him. "'Mornin'. Is this for me?" she asked, pressing her sweet ass against his erection, effectively blowing what little brain cells he'd amassed during his slumber.

CHAPTER TWELVE

"Every inch," he replied next to her ear, kissing her neck while he reached around to fill his hand with one of her lush breasts. His mouth watered at the feel of her stiff peak.

She moaned, and when she pressed back against him again, he saw stars. "I can't believe my body wants more of yours so soon."

He flipped her onto her back to suck her nipple into his mouth, and she responded with another of her sexy-as-hell moans. "Ditto," he murmured against her soft skin as his hand traveled south so he could slip a finger inside.

Hell, yeah.

Need fisted his groin when he found her wet. He drew back to stare down at her flushed face, and her beautiful eyes hazy with need. "Don't think I'll ever get enough of you, Sandy." He skimmed a hand down her throat, over her breasts, lingering on her beaded nipples. *God*, she was beautiful. "Never get enough."

A sensual smile curved her lips and caught his heart. "Ditto." She flung his word back at him while arching into his hand.

And just like that, he was toast. A goner. She had him, but good. Truth be told, Sandy Vickers had gotten under his skin over three years ago.

Switching his attention to her other breast, he bent down to rasp his tongue over her nipple, drawing a hissed breath from her throat. *So responsive.* She arched up, pushing more of her sweet flesh into his mouth. *And so demanding.*

The woman was perfect for him.

Licking and nipping, he continued to answer her wordless demands. Not letting his hand remain idle, he caressed his way south again, running his fingers down her trembling thigh then back up until he found, *ah...yeah...*her slick center.

She was destroying him.

He traced her with the pad of his finger, and she moaned again and rocked into his touch. Back and forth, he outlined her lush folds while he flicked his tongue over her nipple. A second later, she cupped his face and pulled him toward her mouth for a hot, wet, wicked kiss that made him throb. But it wasn't time. No, he was on a mission and refused to be sidetracked from hearing and watching her as he brought her to climax.

Archer stroked her with his finger, and she made a sexy sound in her throat before thrusting her tongue into his mouth as she rocked against his hand.

Fuck, she was hot. *So incredibly hot.* He slid his finger inside her then pulled out on a long, sure stroke. Sandy released his mouth to pant his name.

Yes...that sound... he loved hearing his name on her lips. So he did it again, and again with deliberate, careful, concentration.

"Archer," she panted. "You need to—"

"Take care of you, I know, and I will." He upped the pace and increased the pressure. She was so close. He could tell by the way she trembled that her orgasm was near. "Come for me, Sandy. I want to feel you...watch you...hear you," he urged, adding a second finger, stroking her longer, faster.

"Then...don't stop."

No fucking chance of that. Leaning on his other arm, he watched her intently. His heart clutched at the absolute rapture covering her face—head back, eyes closed, lower lip caught between her teeth while she grasped the sheets with both hands.

God, she was a sight.

Hair wild and fanned out across his pillow, her lush body arched, breasts rippling with her movements. Never had he ever seen anything so damn beautiful. It made him even hotter, pushed his control and he nearly lost it when she gasped out his name and tightened around him as she burst.

Talking himself back from the edge, he stayed with her, bringing her down slowly before he removed his touch. She opened her eyes and gazed at him, her panting filling the space between them.

"Good m-morning...to...me..." Her satisfied smile brought him pleasure unlike any he'd known before. She lifted up to kiss him, before dropping onto her back to suck in more air.

He caressed her jaw and chuckled. "That just one hand."

"Not sure I could survive two," she uttered through her smile.

He leaned down to bite the sweet spot behind her ear, making her cling to him. "Challenge accepted."

"Good. But right now, I'm in need of something else of yours," she said breathlessly, running her hand down his chest to his lower abs, and if she just—

Yeah. Hell, yeah. *That*.

She stroked his erection with one hand and cupped his balls with the other, making him groan and press closer. He wasn't going to last long. Clenching his jaw, he reached for one of the condoms he'd set on his nightstand last night, rooting through the opened packets until he found an unopened one, then kneeled between her legs.

And still, she held on, something unintelligible sounding from her throat as her eyes devoured the part of him she fondled.

The woman was destroying him.

He sucked in a breath. "Sandy..." His voice was rough, because *damn*, he was barely holding the fuck on. He removed her hand, sucking in another breath—or three—while he tore the packet open and rolled on the condom.

Her hand returned to stroke and caress him, and when she sat up to lick his nipple, he hissed in another breath.

"I can't wait to have you inside me, Archer..."

What a coincidence. He couldn't wait to *be* inside the tempting woman.

She settled back on her elbows, staring up at him with so much heat in her eyes, it was a wonder he didn't fucking disintegrate. "I need to feel you," she whispered, spreading her legs wider.

It was his control that disintegrated. With a sound hovering between a groan and a growl, he grabbed her hips, brushed her center with his tip, and plunged into her wetness in one quick, hard thrust.

Oh, fuck...yeah.

A low moan sounded deep in her chest as she closed her eyes. "Feels so good."

So damn good. His grip tightened to hold her still. If she moved even a hair, he was a goner. She must've felt the same because they remained that way for several seconds, seemingly lost in the same ecstasy. It had never felt like this with any other woman. They fit perfectly.

Surrounded by her warmth, he felt consumed, yet whole. Every damn time.

All things that should send up red flags in his head, and yet, none appeared. He didn't care, and he wanted more.

Apparently on the same page, she lifted up to nip his chin, then his lower lip, her glorious breasts and stiff peaks grazing his chest. "Archer..." Her warm breath hit his face, and a shudder racked through her straight into him.

"I know," he managed to reply, his lips brushing hers as he began to move. Slowly at first, but not for long. They were far beyond that pace. And Christ, she felt good. *So damn good.* He'd never felt anything so exquisite.

Joined in the most primal, basic of ways, he closed his eyes and wished he could remain that way...to savor her forever.

When she murmured his name again, Archer opened his eyes to find her staring at him through dark pools of desire, a bounce rippling through her breasts with each thrust. Just like earlier, she was breathtaking. His heart rocked, and *son-of-a-bitch*, a connection powered through him. Sandy glanced down to where they joined, and he watched, too, as he thrust into her, hard.

She trembled around him. It was too much. Nearing the edge, needing to end the sensual climb they'd started, he grabbed her hip and slid her underneath him more, changing the angle before he reached between them to brush his thumb over her center. In an instant, she climaxed, and he immediately followed, her constricting warmth milking him dry.

Spent, breathing hard, he collapsed on top of her. *Christ*, he couldn't feel his bones. Doing his best, he angled his body to the side so he didn't crush her, and worked to catch his breath.

She smiled while panting. "It's a...good morning...now."

He chuckled and kissed her shoulder. "Agreed. Give me a few minutes, and I'll get breakfast started."

She blinked up at him at him. "I'll be happy to help...as soon as I can feel my legs."

He could relate. He was having trouble trying to find his bones.

***

Three and a half hours later, Sandy sat in the nest with the team. It would've been two and a half, but she'd borrowed a shirt, and cash from Archer—after he agreed to let her pay him back—intending to stop at a store to pick up some clothes. Only, the sweetheart took her to the outlets in Atlantic City. That was dangerous, and fruitful. She smoothed her hand over the navy and white stripped sweater, loving the pattern and the feel of the soft material. She'd always been a sucker for all things nautical.

Which, apparently, included her men.

How could she not?

With a name like Sandy, it was practically ordained.

She bit back a grin at her stupid thoughts and glanced around her new temporary headquarters. She found the layout eerily similar to the one that now sat under tons of rubble in Brooklyn. Like that one, the AC base was also hidden in a seemingly abandoned building, but it wasn't by the water. This one sat more inland. The open-concept design was the same, though, with TJ's sanctuary to the right, and stairs to the left that led to bedrooms upstairs.

From what Archer told her, only TJ slept in the nest. Bella and Matteo owned a house on the beach just south of Atlantic City.

Her gaze skimmed over the *bone*frogman who reminded her—with a deep, delicious, intensity—of certain muscles in her body she'd forgotten for years. Heat warmed her veins. Much like the man, the lover side of him was very passionate and giving. Sandy was damn glad they'd decided not to wait to give in to their chemistry. She was sore as a bugger, but it'd been so worth it.

Still silently watching him, she adored how he stood in an at-ease position, arms behind his back, watching a monitor with a live feed of the bank from cameras he and Matteo had installed the other night. A military man through-and-through. The sudden urge to rub against him and climb up his body was so strong, Sandy turned her back to him and focused on the other monitors still running facial recognition on the bald man with the eye tattoo.

"Do you think he had plastic surgery to change his facial features?" she asked no one in particular.

"It's possible," Archer said. "That would explain why we haven't gotten a hit on him yet."

Bella waived at TJ. "*Dude* has a program for that I bet."

TJ nodded. "It's true, I do. I'll start running him through it in a minute. First, though, you're all set, Sandy," the computer guru said, getting up from a chair on her left. "Your hard drive is all rigged up and ready to go on this computer." He drummed the desk. "I also took the liberty of super charging a new laptop for you. It has the latest upgrades, a great video card, not that crap it comes with, my own special security—not even God could get into this now—and I downloaded all the info from your hard drive into it."

She sucked in a breath, her eyes widening at the gleaming laptop also sitting on the desk. "Wow…that's so sweet of you." She walked over to

TJ and pulled him in for a hug. "*You* are the man. Thank you!"

After he turned beet red and sat down in the chair at his station, she ignored the stiffness in her thighs from overexertion last night and stepped over to a smirking Bella to embrace her for the second time that day.

"What this one for?" Bella asked.

"Same thing. For rescuing that hard drive from certain death last night," she replied, releasing the woman to hug Bella's husband again. The thought of anything happening to her neighbors...and the children... "And not just my hard drive, but the whole building. Thank you."

Apparently, there were three booby traps they'd uncovered and removed from her apartment. Bella and TJ were currently running tests on the equipment used for the traps to try to pinpoint a manufacturer, and then possibly a suspect. None of them expected it to go anywhere, but they were following protocol just the same.

"See anything out of the ordinary on our bank feed?" Archer asked.

Matteo shook his head. "No. Nothing."

Archer motioned to the gun on a processing table. "What about the Glock I procured yesterday?"

"As expected, the serial numbers were filed off," Bella replied. "And the only fingerprints are yours."

Running a hand through his hair, Archer expelled a breath. "All three did have gloves on."

She groaned, "My freaking brain is scattered. I took photos of the men who tried to kill us at DHS yesterday. Here." She handed her cell to TJ, who hooked it up to a cable attached to the console.

"I'll start running them through now," he said, clicking each photo to begin the facial recognition process.

She faced the others and grimaced. "Sorry I didn't remember about them sooner."

"Hey," Archer stepped close and rubbed her arm, "I forgot about the photos, too."

Yeah, they were kind of preoccupied last night. Warmth spread through her body at the memories. This was one of those incidents they were worried about with respect to interfering with the job. Hopefully, it wouldn't happen again, or Sandy would nhave to put herself on an Archer time out.

"What about Rodrigo?" Bella asked, and Sandy's chest immediately tightened.

Matteo pinched the bridge of his nose. "It doesn't make sense."

Archer frowned. "What part?"

"All of it," Bella replied.

Sandy was inclined to agree. "It couldn't be a coincidence that he was outside the Federal Reserve Bank with his cart on Monday. Then we ran into him again with his cart near DHS two days later."

"Agreed." He nodded. "New York City has over three thousand vendors, and that's only counting the ones with licenses."

"And both times you ran into the guy, there were attempts on Sandy's life," Bella pointed out.

Her chest squeezed tighter. The thought that the friendly vendor would try to harm her was hard for her brain to compute. But she knew, with proper motivation, a person could do things they never would've ordinarily considered. Perhaps he was being coerced.

Archer grimaced, his mouth drawn into a tight line. "And then he ends up dead in front of your apartment building two hours after that."

Matteo shook his head. "Definitely not a coincidence."

Again, Sandy was inclined to agree. "Have you been able to find anything, TJ?" she asked. "Surely, out of all the cameras in the city, one of them picked up something that would explain that outcome. Who killed Rodrigo and why?"

TJ turned to face her. "I haven't found anything yet, but I haven't given up. I only stopped to get your computers together."

"Thanks. Sorry." She gave a weak smile. "I'm just a little frustrated."

Archer moved close to slip an arm around her shoulder, and the gesture surprised her. Not the fact that he did it, but the fact he did it in private in front of their team, not out in public while pretending to be a couple.

Did that mean they were a couple?

Her heart rocked. She liked him. A lot.

She liked having sex with him, too. A lot.

But she couldn't think beyond that, not with this case seeming to have more questions than answers.

"We can all relate," he said, releasing her arm, frustration lining his face. "According to the feed TJ recorded from Brooklyn last night, I think we can all agree this is the same terror group from Munich."

She nodded with the others. The feed showed Matteo and TJ leaving. Then Bella leaving. Four minutes later, the power went out for eleven minutes before it came back on. A little while later, their SUV arrived just in time for the fireworks.

"It's like someone pointed a device at the building," she said. "Maybe from a safe distance so they remained undetected by TJ's security. And that device disrupted power before this team moved in, killing the prisoners, rigging the place, retreating, then resetting the power." The precision and efficiency scared her.

"Reminds me of a few ops I was on," Bella muttered.

Everyone glanced at the former terrorist hunter. "Not the killing the prisoners part." Bella shrugged. "Mostly."

"Well, this group moves like a military team, and has top-notch equipment," Archer said. "So, we need to up our game. Stay alert. Tighten our security." He turned his attention to TJ. "Could they have gotten any information from your computers?"

TJ scowled and shook his head. "No way. Like I said, not even God can get through my security."

"You're sure?"

"*Absatively.*" TJ nodded. "I've already run diagnostics to see if any files had been accessed and it's a big negatory, boss."

Archer blew out a breath. "I hope you're right."

"So, you think it's the rogue group from Munich that's after Sandy, and not someone unrelated to the case," Matteo stated, not asked. "Is it because you two were spotted doing recon on Monday? Or because DHS has her working this case?"

"I don't know." Archer shook his head. "Could be both."

"Because otherwise, it makes no sense," Matteo said.

She turned to him. "I've been thinking about that. Perhaps because it makes no sense...it makes perfect sense."

Archer narrowed his eyes. "What do you mean?"

She lifted a hand and waved at the monitors that showed the bank, DHS, the Munich bombing, the outside of her apartment building, and their Brooklyn headquarters. "All of these seemingly unrelated bizarre happenings might be just that. Unrelated, bizarre happenings," she said. "Except they do have a common thread. Me."

TJ smirked. "Okay. Think we already knew that."

She turned to him and quirked a brow. "True...but *why* me?"

"Because we must've stumbled onto something, or someone, on our recon Monday evening," Archer said.

"Possibly," she said. "But you were there, too, and they haven't exactly targeted you."

A smile tugged his lips. "That's because they couldn't find me...well, other than at headquarters, but then they did try to kill me."

"They tried to kill us all," Bella corrected.

"Because they'd caught a break," she stated. "But before that, it's possible they were targeting me to get your focus off your job of stopping this supposed attack." She met each of their gazes one at a time. "Instead, you're running around the city trying to keep me safe and investigate who is trying to kill me."

Archer uttered a curse. "So...what are you saying?"

"I'm saying we need to stop doing that." They were wasting time and manpower.

TJ's brows shot up. "Stop keeping you safe?"

"Yes...well, no." She shook her head.

"Good." Archer lifted a hand to cup her face. "Because no way in hell is that going to stop."

She smiled and turned her face until her lips brushed his palm before she drew back. "What I'm saying is, I'm safe here, so I'll stay put, and you won't have to worry about me anymore. I can work from my computer anywhere. So that's what I'll do, and you can go back to tracking down those involved in the threat to the bank."

He nodded. "Maybe you're right. Maybe all that chaos was to throw me off their scent. But it also means they were involved in everything that happened to you, so it's that much more evidence we have to comb through to try to identify them."

"Starting with those dead guys at DHS," TJ said, pointing to one of the photos. "We have a positive ID on one. A Gregor Uscinski. Former Russian military. Dishonorable discharge."

"They were military?" She frowned. The attack on their Brooklyn headquarters, sure, but the stairwell? "The way Archer took them down with such ease, I find that hard to believe. Was it because he surprised them?"

Bella's laugh echoed her husband's. "No, it's because Archer is that good. He made them look like idiots because he's elite and they weren't."

She glanced at Archer and he shrugged. Sandy knew he was elite. She also knew he was too humble to boast. "Were you able to determine if the prisoners had tracking devices injected under their skin?" she asked.

Bella shook her head. "No. We couldn't tell from the feed. It's possible their skin had already healed."

"What about Jimmy?" Archer turned his attention to Matteo. "What did you find out about him?"

The other former SEAL leaned back against the console and folded his arms across his chest. "Entry level position. Nothing special. I'm guessing he was their way of accessing inside."

Accessing what?

She frowned. "So why kill him?"

Matteo and Bella both shook their heads.

"Not sure," Archer replied. "But there was definitely a reason. This rogue team doesn't make a move unless there's a reason."

She cocked her head. "So, where does that leave us? What do we do next? Should I try to investigate the DHS mole?" Her mind told her it was someone she knew, which made her heart heavy.

"No." Archer shook his head. "Silas is on it. Let it be."

She nodded.

"Matteo and I are going to check out Rodrigo's apartment," Archer said. "See if that's where…if there are any clues there."

It wasn't lost on Sandy that he stopped himself from saying something that might upset her. His thoughtfulness was truthfully mind-blowing. Not that she thought of military men as brutes, but they didn't come across as thoughtful, either. So, to see this side of Archer, and having it directed at her was...well...mind-blowing.

Matteo straightened from the console. "Roger that."

"And Sandy and I are going shopping." Bella hooked her arm through hers and tugged her toward the door.

Sandy glanced down at her beloved sweater. "What's wrong with what I'm wearing?"

"Nothing." The woman grinned. "I freaking love it. I want one before they're all gone."

An hour later, Sandy discovered what Bella meant by shopping, was buying that sweater on their way to a local bar full of patrons with ties to the New York City.

They were on a fishing expedition.

CHAPTER THIRTEEN

Nodding to the waitress who dropped off drinks Bella had ordered while she'd stopped at the restroom, Sandy eyed the two glasses of...wine?

"So, I take it we're fishing...and drinking?"

Bella grinned. "That's to help your muscles relax."

Muscles relax?

"Why?" She frowned.

What in the world was the former terrorist hunter planning to do?

"Because I can tell you're sore. Trust me. I remember my first all-nighter with Matteo. I could barely walk." A dreamy look entered her eyes. "It was great." The woman sighed and reached for her wine. "The sore muscles afterward...not so much. So, drink up. Trust me, it'll help."

Ignoring the surge of heat sweeping into her face, Sandy sipped her wine in order to avoid replying.

"And now that we're here." Bella grinned. "I'd love to know what you think about those two men in the corner."

Big mouth trouble makers. "Not my type."

Bella snorted. "Obviously. You're dating Captain America, why would you dally with a Dillinger wannabe?"

Sandy smiled at the woman comparing Archer to the same superhero she had the other day.

"I mean, use your superpowers and tell me what you see about them." Bella nodded her head toward the corner while lifting her glass to her lips.

Superpowers? Cute. Her lips twitched.

"Okay." Sipping more wine, she eyed the men in question. "Scrappy, college educated—two years, not four—but enough to make them think they're better than their peers. They belong to a club." They thought they were tough, and because of it they didn't bother to keep their voices down. They wore suits, signet rings, expensive haircuts but drank cheap booze, sported identical tattoos on their right pinkies. She stilled. Right pinkie? "Wait...their tattoos are street cred for smuggling someone into the country." She recognized them from research on an old DA case.

"Thought so." Bella nodded, her back still to the men. "Over a year ago, Matteo and I worked a case where someone was smuggling terrorists in via the ocean to bomb New York."

Sandy sucked in a breath. "Times Square. New Year's Eve," she muttered. "I picked up the chatter and forwarded it through channels. You were the one called in?"

Bella grinned. "Yes, well, me and Matteo, but for separate reasons."

Judging by the derision in the woman's eyes, Sandy guessed it meant the two hadn't been on the same page. Damn. That had to be interesting.

"Anyway," Bella continued, "I had a hunch those two were into smuggling, and you've confirmed my suspicions that I'm barking up the right twig."

She raised a brow. "Twig? Don't you mean tree?"

Bella snickered. "Not with their scrawny bodies. But I suspect they may know something helpful about this case, if those Munich...*people* didn't come into the country legally."

"Good idea." She nodded. "Should I call Archer?"

Bella finished her wine and shook her head. "No. He and Matteo are probably halfway to the city by now. I can handle this." The woman dug keys from her pocket and handed them to Sandy. "Take the vehicle. I'll find my own way back. I'd ask you to join the fun, but I think *Cap* would kill me."

About to correct the woman over Archer being a former commander not a captain, she realized it was a comic book reference again. "Okay," she said. "Try not to enjoy yourself too much."

"Not making any promises." Bella winked, before tossing money on the table. "Drink's on me," she said, rising to her feet with Sandy.

Deciding not to even contemplate what was about to take place, she headed back to the nest, eager to check for chatter. She'd been a little busy the past two days to do so, and her gut told her to get on it. Starting with chatter right here in Atlantic City.

***

Archer went with his gut and decided it was best if they kept Jimmy's death a secret from the man's supervisor, at least for another twenty-four to forty-eight hours. Just in case someone made a move to use the man's computer or desk. TJ had an isolated feed on it.

He put off calling the Federal Reserve for the time being and headed to Hell's Kitchen to check out Rodrigo's apartment.

Murdered by two gunshots to the chest. That much was certain. But he wanted to know if the young vendor had anything to do with this Munich bunch, and he was determined to find out.

Pretending to be reporters, Archer was surprised by the cooperation most of the people gave Matteo and him. They started with Rodrigo's roommate, thrilled when the man invited them inside.

While Matteo asked questions, Archer videotaped the interview, getting good footage of the apartment. "I still can't believe it," the young Asian said. "*Rodro* was just telling me he was invited to a good spot this week. He was excited because that doesn't happen often."

"Where is his cart?" Matteo asked. "What will happen to it?"

The roommate shrugged. "His cart is in a garage in Midtown. I don't know what will happen to it. His parents already came and cleared out all his stuff. Maybe they got his cart, too. I hope they did and lease the license to earn some money to pay for the funeral."

Archer knew there was big money in leasing vendor licenses, he also knew it was possible the cart was already stolen. There was big money in that as well.

"Do you know which garage?" Matteo asked. "Maybe we can help?"

"No. Sorry." The guy shook his head. "I think it was near the museum. It wasn't too far from here because he usually got home pretty quick once the flatbed dropped his cart at the garage."

After leaving the apartment, he sent a text to TJ to check one of the photos Sandy took of the cart to get the license number and see if he could track down which garage it might be stored in. Then they started to canvas the neighbors, surprised to find them talkative, instead of tight-lipped. It appeared *Rodro* was well-liked. Although, there'd been plenty of homegrown terrorists who'd shocked family and friends when they were discovered. And at least one person didn't like the vendor since he had two bullets in him.

"I think he was offed for his cart," one of the neighbors said.

Another disagreed. "Nah, it was just a mugging. I heard he was robbed, too. Only an empty wallet left on his chest."

Archer had read the police report, and the wallet rumor was correct. It was still undetermined where Rodrigo had been killed, though. No signs of struggle or large amounts of blood at the scene, so it'd been ruled a dumping ground. His apartment had been ruled out as the scene of the crime, too.

He was liking this Midtown garage more and more for the murder scene. Hopefully, TJ would come up with an address soon. In the meantime, they continued to knock on doors.

A third neighbor suggested aliens, then got into an argument with his brother, who'd insisted it was lizard people who came out of the sewer.

And another neighbor suggested a drug deal gone bad. "Although, I ain't never seen Rodro do drugs, ya know. I'm thinking someone wanted to pedal them through his cart and when he refused, they shot him."

Archer videotaped, while Matteo took notes and after two hours of canvasing the area, and a trip to the garage at the address TJ sent, they decided to head back to New Jersey.

Rodrigo's vendor cart was indeed missing. No blood spatters visible from the doorway. TJ was already viewing footage of the area. Guilty or innocent, Rodrigo would have justice either way.

"So," Matteo said when they were a few minutes away from headquarters and conversation about the case lulled. "You taking Sandy back to your place again tonight? Or will she be staying at the nest with TJ?"

He snapped his gaze to the man smirking at him from the passenger seat and debated on whether or not he needed to wipe the smirk off his buddy's face.

"Ah…" Matteo scratched the bridge of his nose, smile still present. "It's like that, is it?"

"What's that supposed to mean?" He tightened his grip on the steering wheel.

"Hey, no offense, sir." His buddy held up his hands. "I think it's great. I'm happy for you. Sandy is nice. I like her."

She was more than nice. She was smart. Beautiful. Tenacious—especially when she…

Archer stopped mid-thought when he realized he'd been thinking out loud.

Shit.

Matteo chuckled. "Don't sweat it, sir. I understand. No one knows messed-up headspace because of a woman better than I do. Trust me. Bella can annihilate my train of thought with just a glance. And if she smiles?" His buddy whistled and shook his head. "Goodbye, brain cells." The smile remained on the seasoned SEAL's face the whole time. "And you know what, sir? I wouldn't change a fucking thing."

Archer nodded and blew out a breath as he turned down the street where headquarters was located. "I'd planned to wait until this mission was over before starting something. I wanted to talk to her son first," he admitted on another exhale. He owed his fellow SEAL that much.

"Get his blessing." Matteo nodded. "I don't think he's going to have a problem with his mother being happy. And you definitely make her happy, sir. Anyone can see her face lights up when you walk in a room."

He'd noticed that, too. It made him feel ten foot tall and off-kilter. "I'm still trying to come to terms with this loss of control aspect, because I sure as shit don't seem to have it when she's around." He pulled into the garage at the nest and parked. "Will it ever come back?"

"God, I hope not." Matteo grinned.

Archer snickered. "It is pretty fuckin' great."

"Hooyah," Matteo spouted, and they were both smiling when they entered the building.

TJ was in the kitchen area, standing by the center island, popping nuked pizza rolls into his mouth. As soon as he saw them, he straightened. "You two are in good moods. I hope it stays that way when you hear what happened."

Archer's heart kicked the shit out of his ribs.

"And before you say anything," TJ held up his hands, "I want you to know I tried to stop them."

"Fuck," Matteo muttered. "What did Bella do now?"

A pained look crossed TJ's face. "It...ah...actually wasn't Bella. This time," he said before he met Archer's gaze. "It was Sandy."

Apparently done beating his ribs, Archer's heart dropped to the floor then shot up to thump in his throat. "What about her?" Cracking his fisted knuckles, he strode right to the guy. "Where is she?"

"On the boardwalk. I think."

"What the fuck for?" He glanced at the clock on the microwave, and pain instantly stabbed at his temples. It was almost twenty-one hundred.

"She got a lead and needed to act on it."

That was great. Fucking great.

He tried to suck air into his lungs but didn't have much luck. "And you let her go alone?" What if that threat in New York *did* manage to follow them here?

"Of course not." TJ reeled back. "Bella's with her."

Now his chest hurt. Squeezing pains ringed his damn chest.

Was he having a heart attack?

"That's supposed to make me feel better?" He glanced at Matteo and lifted a shoulder. "No offense, man."

Matteo held up his hands. "None taken. I'm a bit freaked out myself."

Fuck. Now his chest really squeezed tight. Rubbing at the ache with one hand, he yanked his phone out of his pocket with the other.

"What are you doing?" TJ frowned and lunged for the phone. "*Nonononono*. Don't call her."

Archer maneuvered the phone high and away, a little surprised at how quick the skinny guy moved. "Why the fuck not?"

"Because you don't want to give up her position."

The pain squeezing his head increased, momentarily messing with his vision.

A stroke…he was having a stroke.

Sandy was somewhere on the boardwalk. At night. Following a lead. With Bella…the agent who killed first and asked questions later.

Archer tried to draw air into his lungs, but his chest was too damn tight.

A stroke *and* a coronary. Could he have them both at the same time?

He was about to fucking find out because the heart lodged in his throat was pounding like a son-of-a-bitch and cutting off the oxygen to his brain.

"A'ight. Time out," Matteo said, thrusting a glass of what smelled like scotch into Archer's hand. "Sir, drink up." Then thrust a finger at TJ. "Spill it. Where are the women exactly, and why?"

"Make it the short version," Archer growled, before tossing back the contents of his glass. The alcohol burned as it slid down his throat and dislodged his thudding heart. For a brief moment, he contemplated locating the bottle.

TJ popped a pizza roll into his mouth and chewed before talking. "Sandy was listening to the chatter here, in AC."

Matteo's head jerked back. "Here?"

"In Atlantic City?" He frowned.

"Yeah." TJ nodded. "That's what *here, in AC* means. Anyhow, she heard talk about FRB. Bomb. And boss."

"Boss?" Matteo frowned. "What boss?"

TJ shrugged. "That's what she went to find out."

Archer expelled a breath and counted to three. "Where?"

"I don't know. Caesars or Bally's maybe..." TJ chewed on another roll. "The prisoners had dealings with some of the whales at Bally's, so my money is on there."

Prisoners?

Archer liked the kid, but he was two seconds away from grabbing TJ by the throat. Instead, he gripped his empty glass with one hand and thrust the other into his pocket to keep from choking

Jameson Knight's computer guru. "What prisoners?"

"Oh, did I forget to mention them?"

Jameson could probably find another guru.

TJ went to reach for another pizza roll but there weren't any left because Matteo swiped the plate and tossed it in the trash in one smooth motion.

"Prisoners?" Archer arched a brow.

"Bella rounded up two smugglers—of people, *people smugglers*—from a local bar."

His heart knocked his ribs, as déjà vu flashed through his mind. "And she brought them here?"

"Yeah. But don't worry." TJ waved a hand. "The dudes have nothing *on* their skin or *under* it. We checked good this time." The guy grimaced. "It wasn't pretty."

"So why did they have to go to a casino?" Matteo asked.

"They were trying to decide which one had the better rooftop for listening." TJ cocked his head. "Oh, yeah, they took one of my drones with them."

Jesus...

Matteo splashed a SEAL-sized shot of scotch into Archer's glass, one for himself in another glass, and together they downed their drinks.

"Don't worry about me," TJ said. "I don't need a drink."

Matteo thrust the bottle at the guy. "Help yourself. And if that was the simple version, I'd hate to hear the long one."

Archer's chest was no longer as tight, and the pounding in his head had lessened to a dull roar. But his temperature was still one notch below incinerator, so he stripped off his button-down shirt and set it on a chair. Feeling instantly cooler in his black muscle shirt, he turned to Matteo. "Let's roll."

It wasn't that he didn't trust Sandy to do her job or Bella to keep Sandy safe, because he trusted them both. Implicitly.

The reason he and Matteo were heading out was to have their women's six. He didn't like them out there without backup.

CHAPTER FOURTEEN

Fifteen minutes later, Archer stood on the boardwalk with Matteo, between Bally's and Caesars, and sent Sandy a text. MATTEO AND I ARE HERE. TEXT ME YOUR LOCATION.

A second later, his phone rang.

It was Sandy. Thank Christ. "We're on Bally's rooftop, but hurry, you need to get to the mall on the pier across from Caesars! The boss...I think he's at the back getting into a boat. We only have a short-range drone. Bella has it hovering near there, but it won't be able to follow him if he gets in a boat."

Shit.

"Okay," he told her and hung up, heading toward the mall at a dead run, filling Matteo in on the way.

Shaped like a cruise ship, the mall was built on a pier...and about to close. They made it inside and sprinted through the nearly vacant halls, bursting through the doors to the observation deck at the back, guns drawn.

But it was empty.

"Shit," Matteo muttered, echoing Archer's thoughts.

The faint roar of a motor boat echoed in the distance, but the night was overcast, and with clouds covering the moon, it was nearly pitch black over the ocean.

He couldn't see a damn thing.

Thrusting a hand through his hair he muttered a curse. "Not again."

If the man disappearing into the night was *the boss* from the chatter, it was possible Archer had just missed the bastard responsible for Munich. Gritting his teeth, he holstered his gun and prayed he'd have another shot at the guy soon.

The phone in his pocket began to vibrate. He fished it out and answered.

"Did you get there in time?" Sandy asked.

"No." *Son-of-a-bitch.* "Tell me you caught sight of him on the drone." They needed a damn photo of this guy.

He glanced over the edge of the pier, noting it was almost a two-story drop to the water. Good. He hoped the bastard had broken his ankle getting into the boat.

"Possibly." She didn't sound as confident as he'd hoped. "He wore a baseball hat and a hoodie over it. Guy's good at shadowing his face. We lost him, so we're making our way down to the boardwalk now. We'll meet you outside the Wild West Casino."

"Roger that." He hung up and filled Matteo in, swallowing another curse as they made their way back to the boardwalk.

They were so close...

Maybe when they viewed the drone footage, they'd find a good enough angle on the guy to run facial recognition. He held onto that thought, and his spirits lifted further when he spotted Sandy coming out of the casino with Bella.

He inhaled and his whole body seemed to sigh at the sight of her unharmed. At least he hadn't found her in one of the gunfight scenarios that had tormented his mind back at the nest.

She'd been doing surveillance. No guns involved.

As she weaved around the small throng of people, turning several male heads along the way, the interest in her eyes and the smile that lit up her face were directed solely at him. The last of the tension in his body disappeared, replaced by a rush of warmth.

He strode across the boardwalk, vaguely aware of Matteo pulling Bella into his arms, as he met Sandy halfway. "Hi," he said, setting his hands on her hips, loving how hers automatically went to his chest. Intending to take just a small kiss, he bent down to brush her lips with his, but the instant his mouth touched hers, his body changed the rules.

Tightening his hold, he kissed her deeply, her hands warm on his skin as they slid up to fist his hair. Blame it on adrenaline from the last half hour, or his concern for her over the past hour, but longing and hunger burst through his body, mixing to form a fierce need to strip them naked and thrust deep inside her.

Whistles and cheers, and even some clapping made it past the fog in his brain, and he forced himself to break the kiss, promising to pick up where they left off when they were alone.

And not in public.

Damn…he was acting like a froglet fresh out of BUD/S.

"Sorry," he said between breaths, kissing her forehead. "Didn't mean for that to get so out of hand."

She chuckled against his neck, her breath warm on his skin. "I did. Still learning how to handle adrenaline, I guess."

He smiled and drew back to stare into her flushed face. God, she was beautiful. "Don't feel you need to on my account."

"Duly noted." She grinned, smoothing his hair before setting her hands back on his chest. "But I'd rather wait until we're at your place."

"Duly noted," he repeated her words back to her, and received another gorgeous smile from the woman he was beginning to realize owned his heart.

"Then we're of accord. We'll continue this later," she said, moving to his side to slide an arm around him. "But first, it's back to the nest so we can fill each other in on today's events."

He nodded. It was time for SITREPs, and to view the drone footage.

And fifteen minutes later, when they convened in the cyber sanctuary, Archer was pleased to see TJ had the footage already up on one of the monitors.

"So far, I've only found a partial of the man, but his face is in the shadows." TJ shook his head. "It's too bad it was dark out."

Bella dropped into a chair. "Think that was his plan."

Archer turned to Sandy. "What makes you think he's the one referred to as *the boss* from the Federal Reserve threats?"

She turned face him. "Because the guys Bella rounded up told us some badass from overseas snuck in near Cape May and was willing to pay top dollar to slip into New York unnoticed tonight."

Shit.

"Through the guys you apprehended?" Matteo asked.

"No," Bella replied, examining her fingernails. "They're too low level. It required someone with bigger connections. So, we decided to take a drone and hit the roof at Bally's, since that's the casino favored by the whales who are the source of the information provided by the two Dillinger wannabees in the back."

Sandy nodded. "And I picked up some clear chatter between two men...one was careful not to talk too much. Give me a second to find it." She glanced at the notes on her phone, flicked a few buttons on the console, fast forwarding the tape to a certain time stamp, then hit play.

Audio of a man claiming to have a speed boat at the back of the pier ready to take him to the rendezvous point filled the room, along with the other man's one word response—"Good."

Archer's heart dropped into his gut. "It's him. I recognize that bastard's voice." He clenched his jaw and fought to keep memories from the past at bay.

In Munich, Archer had heard the bomber laugh over the com line and state, "Too late" a second before the bomb went off.

He'd never forget that voice or the laugh.

"I won't let him set off another bomb," he muttered through clenched teeth.

A warm hand glided down his arm and curled over his fist, easing his fingers open. "Tell us what we need to know about him and his team."

"His team is small. Three to four, max," Archer said. "We think he uses outside muscle to do preliminary footwork, but we're not certain, because they're never found."

"Like two guys with their throats cut, buried under tons of rubble," Bella said.

Shit.

"Yeah, exactly like that." He nodded.

"And another with two bullets to the chest," Matteo added.

Rodrigo...

Archer felt Sandy stiffen, so he lightly squeezed her hand. "The circumstances surrounding his murder are unclear," he told her quietly.

"Yeah," TJ said. "I'm still searching through Midtown footage. I'll find something. I know it."

Sandy nodded. "Thanks. Do you want help?"

"No. I'm good." TJ wisely turned her down.

Archer glanced at the live feed from the cameras he and Matteo had set up at the other night. "Any activity at the Reserve?"

"Nothing. It's all quiet, too," TJ replied. "I'll let you know if that changes. I've set up alarms to alert me at the slightest quiver."

Good.

"Do you think he'll jump right in and try to set bombs tonight?" Sandy asked.

Archer shook his head. "No. He knows he's being watched and has to assume the Reserve is too. He's going to case things for a few days."

"Any chance he'll think it's too risky and leave?" She glanced up at him.

"Bastard likes a challenge." Archer intended to rise to it this time.

New York had already seen too much damage at the hands of lunatics and Archer wasn't about to allow another one to destroy any more lives and change the landscape again.

***

An hour later, after making plans to meet again in the morning, Archer left with Sandy, but instead of heading home, he drove them to the marina. The moon was visible now and the reflection off the ocean drew him in.

He parked in the lot and turned to face her. "You up for a moonlight cruise?"

"Yes." Her smile was visible from the dashboard light. "I've never been on a boat at night."

He cut the engine and grinned. "There's nothing like it."

And he was excited to share the experience with her…and to be the first one to take her out at night.

After he helped her on board and cast off, Archer realized she was the only person, besides Silas, to be on his boat. *His* sanctuary. His escape from the world. And as he piloted them out on the ocean at night, it was as if they were the only two people in the world. A private haven. Exactly where he wanted her.

Careful to anchor a few miles off shore in a protected area, not in a shipping lane, he flicked on more than just the anchor light. Last thing Archer wanted was an inexperienced yahoo hitting them and ruining their night.

"This is amazing," she said, coming back upstairs to the help area to join him after exploring the stateroom and head below at his urging. Smiling, she turned her back to the galley and dinette area and stood next to him, by the pilot chair. "And the moon...it's like a streetlight," she said, gazing out the window. "It's so clear out here. So beautiful."

He cut the engine and tugged her onto his lap. "Very beautiful," he murmured, cupping her face with his free hand, while the other cupped the curve of her gorgeous ass. He leaned forward and kissed her softly on the lips, nipping and tasting, taking his time to savor her sweetness.

When he drew back, she was trembling in his arms, and Archer wasn't sure he'd ever felt so at peace. His soul was in a good place. Where it should always be.

Where it was meant to be.

"Thanks for bringing me out here." She stared down at him, her gaze reflecting her soft tone.

He leaned forward and kissed the tip of her nose. "Thanks for coming."

A wicked grin spread across her lips. "But I haven't...yet."

His dick immediately stirred. "Challenge accepted."

She ran her hands up his chest to rest on his shoulders. "Roger that."

His lips twitched as he lowered them to brush hers. Once. Twice. Then full-on as he kissed her slow and deep and thorough, making sure she knew he planned to please.

It hit him then. This kiss, this embrace was different than any they'd shared. Just as hot, but…more, powerful, demanding everything from him, all he had. It was soul-searching and intense.

Perfect.

If it wasn't for the fact he needed air, Archer never would've broken it. He banded his arms around her as they both worked to catch their breath. He was a lucky son-of-a-bitch. It boggled his mind that someone so amazing, so special, enjoyed his company.

When this mission was over, he needed to travel down to Virginia Beach to talk to her son, because he didn't ever want to let her go.

Sandy stirred in his lap, brushing his body with her warm, soft curves, making his heart beat hard against his ribs. Then she leaned in and brushed her mouth to his ear. "Archer?"

He let out a shaky breath. "Yeah?"

"I have a present to give you."

He drew back to meet her gaze. "You, here with me…that's a gift, Sandy. I don't need anything else."

Her gaze was soft and warm…and growing wicked as she slipped off his lap and turned the pilot chair, with him in it, until there was more room in front of him. "I bought you a little something on my shopping spree today." The promise in her words tripped his pulse, but when she grabbed the hem of her sweater and yanked it over her head—in a hot-as-hell move he'd remember to his grave—she revealed the sexiest damn bra he'd ever seen.

It was navy blue with her nipples playing peek-a-boo through a patch of lace he wanted to remove with his teeth.

Then she unhooked her jeans, and slowly drew the zipper down, inflating the boner in his pants to epic size by the time she stepped out of her jeans and stood in front of him in her sexy bra and matching lace panties.

Archer sucked in a breath and would've told her how incredible she looked and how much he loved his present, but all the blood had drained out of his dehydrated brain to settle in his groin, temporarily robbing him of speech.

"Do you like it?" she asked, doing a slow twirl-around that literally stopped his heart for several beats.

The lace was shaped in a vee, affording him an incredible view of her sweet cheeks, and he wanted to remove that lace with his teeth as well.

"Fuck, Sandy," he muttered, his voice sounding low and rough with the need coursing through his body, no longer suppressed from their earlier boardwalk embrace.

She smirked. "I'm counting on it."

Damn…he loved her wit.

Archer laughed and knew if he wasn't careful, he could so easily fall in love with the woman.

Ah…who the hell was he trying to fool? He was more than halfway in love with her already.

She sauntered close…which was good, considering he was too hard to move without bursting the damn seams of his jeans.

"I sure hope you have a condom," she said, straddling him on the chair, in a move that nearly caused him to swallow his tongue.

But he could still smile…and talk. "I have two."

"Hooyah," she whispered, slipping her hands under his shirt to slowly push it up his body, her fingers grazing his skin in feather-light touches that drove him mad. "My ever-prepared frogman."

A thrill shot down his body over the possessive word that matched the gleam in her eyes. "Always," he told her, and when she tried to push his shirt over his head, he helped her remove it all the way with a quick tug, then dropped it on top of her clothes on the floor.

She smiled. "Thank you."

"Anytime." Forcing himself to behave, he set his hands lightly on her hips, letting her call the shots, to see what she had planned for him.

Her hands made a slow pass up his arms, over his shoulders, and down his body, brushing leisurely over his abs. "Mmm…you're so hard and hot," she murmured in response to the feel of him, like maybe she couldn't get enough of him. And as if to prove it, she bent low and licked his nipple, but before his hissed breath finished echoing through the helm, she straightened and gently touched her lips to his.

"Sandy—" He tightened his grip on her hips, as his entire body reacted to that light, sweet kiss.

"I know." She outlined his lower lip with her tongue.

He groaned, and unable to remain immobile any longer, he sucked it into his mouth. Damn...he loved the taste of her, the feel of her. He'd never get enough. Gliding his hands up her sides, he skimmed her breasts and brushed his thumbs over her lace-covered nipples. She moaned, and he shoved a hand in her hair, while he ran his other down her back to cup a handful of her sweet, sweet ass.

"I want you," she whispered against his lips.

Fuck...he wanted her too.

He made a noise deep in his throat and kissed her long and slow. He needed more—needed to touch her. All of her. With his mouth still on hers, he ran both his hands up and down her body and felt her every inhale and delicious tremor. They were so close he felt her heart rock.

His rocked too.

"Sandy," he murmured, releasing her mouth to kiss a path down her jaw, her throat, and nip at her collarbone, then soothed it with his tongue. Goosebumps broke out over her skin and her nipples pebbled behind the navy lace. His mouth watered. Damn, he needed to taste her. Dragging his mouth over her cleavage, he felt her breath hitch, while he reached around to unhook the bra keeping her curves intact. Straightening his back, he slid a finger under each strap, then met her dark, heated gaze as he slowly tugged them down her arms.

The rapid rise and fall of her chest helped his plight to free her breasts. He pulled the lace off and tossed it over his shoulder, and the sexy woman moaned before his mouth even covered her tight peak. Damn...he smiled against her skin. She was so responsive.

Sandy had her hands in his hair, and her body arched in a sweet offering Archer gladly accepted, teasing one nipple with his mouth and tongue, while he caught the other between his forefinger and thumb.

Her moan washed over him, echoing through the helm while her rocking nearly did him the fuck in. He saw stars, as she continued to rain sweet torture on his tense body. But he wasn't the only one on edge. Still nuzzling her chest, he slid both hands down her body, tugged the small scrap of lace aside to find her spread wide open and soaking wet.

His heart rocked hard and his erection pulsed. He glanced down. Fuck, she was breathtaking.

She half gasped, half moaned, so he stroked her again. "Archer...yes...more."

Not a problem. He was too addicted. "Yes, ma'am." He loved to please her. Loved her reactions, so he stroked and brushed different spots, different angles, watching her face while she gripped the arms of the chair, leaning back while arching into his touch.

"Archer...yeah...there—" She rocked harder.

Completely lost in her beauty and the way she took pleasure in him, he thrilled in her moans and little pants and each sexy sound he ripped from her throat. Tension coiled in her tight. She was ready to snap.

She was the most beautiful woman he'd ever seen.

Wanting to give her what she needed, he lengthened his strokes, and added the brush of his thumb while he leaned forward to capture a bouncing nipple in his mouth and graze the tight peak with his teeth.

Her low, throaty moan vibrated through him, as she shattered and nearly sent him over the edge with her.

He brought her down slowly, and when he eventually removed his touch, she slumped against him. Giving her time to find her breath, he trailed a hand up her back and into her hair to tip her face so he could kiss her quick.

Damn…satisfaction tasted so good on her.

Drawing back, he stared into her warm gaze while he slowly helped her to stand so he could remove the rest of his lacy present from her lush body.

She trembled before him. "Please hand me a condom and get naked."

CHAPTER FIFTEEN

Roger that.

He stood, fished a condom from his pocket and handed it to her before stripping out of the rest of his clothes.

"My ever-prepared SEAL," she murmured, pushing him back down into the chair and stood before him wearing nothing but a hungry, possessive look in her gorgeous blue eyes.

He was a dead man.

And Archer nearly did expire when Sandy held his gaze and ripped the packet open with her teeth, then insisted on sheathing him, using two wicked hands to slowly roll on the condom, squeezing and stroking in all the right places, leaving him out of breath and sweating.

He throbbed in her hands and swallowed a curse, trying desperately to hold on. "Sandy—"

"I need you in me, Archer."

Christ, the urgency and hunger in her tone didn't help.

"Now, please…" Sure of herself and begging— about the sexiest combination he'd ever fucking seen. Then she straddled him again, grasped him with one hand and lined them up before she slowly sank down and took him in deep.

"Ah…damn…Sandy," he muttered through clenched teeth.

"Mmm…" Her moan vibrated around him.

Fuck.

He closed his eyes and talked himself back from the edge. Then she leaned in and nipped at his neck. In a swift move, he wrapped an arm around her and thrust his hips, burying himself even deeper inside her lush heat.

"God, Archer…" Now *she* hissed out a breath, then moaned when he ran his hands lightly down her thighs.

Holding her smoldering gaze, he caressed her hot curves, reaching behind her to cup her sweet ass. Then he began to move. Slow and long, lifting her up while he pulled nearly all the way out, then pushing in deep, until his eyes wanted to cross.

"God, you feel so good." He felt her everywhere. They were chest to chest, thigh to thigh, not a speck of air between them.

"So do you," she murmured softly, rocking her body to meet his thrusts. "So good."

Too good. The need and hunger took over. He upped the pace. Faster. Harder. Spurred on by her sexy panting and moans, he gave her everything he had, let her see everything he felt. And he felt a hell of a lot. Lost, falling, found, and he saw the very same crazy, consuming emotions in her eyes. She was as gone as he. As completely undone, and off-kilter, and the knowledge he was making her feel those things too, made him feel like the luckiest man alive.

"Archer," she breathed, brushing her lips over his.

He took over the kiss, taking everything, giving more.

She bucked and made sweet noises in her throat, and when he reached between their bodies and pressed his thumb above where they connected, she squeezed his shoulders and broke the kiss. He watched as she cried out his name while tightening around him. It was too much and exactly right. He slid his hands to her hips and held her there as he thrust one last, deep thrust inside her and joined her in a release so powerful, he momentarily lost his vision, and definitely lost his head. And his heart.

And as he came with the amazing, beautiful, giving woman, Archer understood. He realized what he'd been missing his whole life, and what he could never live without again.

He would do what he had to…do whatever it took. He was going to fight to keep her in his life.

***

An hour later, Sandy snuggled closer to the sexy furnace keeping her warm under a blanket while they cuddled on the bench cushions on the deck of his boat gazing up at the moon and stars above. She knew they were going to head back to shore soon, but what they'd shared inside was so hot and wild and amazing this night would always be an incredibly special memory for her.

And she'd never look at a pilot seat the same way ever again. Archer was a great pilot. Great at driving things. He'd piloted them out to a beautiful spot…and her body with perfection and precision while he drove her out of her mind. A smile tugged her lips.

She was out to sea with her SEAL...

Was he her SEAL?

Was Archer the type to *be* someone's SEAL?

She'd like to think he wanted that with her. The way he looked at her with both longing and adoration the past few days gave her hope that it could happen, if they let it.

But they lived in two different states. He'd retired from a life of saving the world, and she was pushing further into that kind of life.

Still...they only lived a few hours apart...and he had done a job or two for an agency that sometimes saved the world. Perhaps they could fit a relationship into the mix...

She hugged the strong arms he had banded around her and sighed. Even if they parted ways at the end of the mission, she was determined to enjoy tonight.

"Keep that up and I'll give you a reason to sigh," he muttered against her ear before sinking his teeth in the curve of her neck.

She immediately sucked in a breath and pressed back against him. "You're on." And to make sure he understood what she wanted, Sandy wiggled her butt, too.

He muttered something under his breath, and a second later, she found herself flat on her back on the cushions with him kneeling above her. "Now, I'm on. Well, almost," he said, slipping out from under the covers to disappear inside a few seconds, before returning with the other condom packet in his hand.

Her pulse leapt and heat flickered through her body. She lifted up to lean back on her elbows and watch his approach, moonlight casting shadows in all his delicious ridges. Her gaze roamed over his magnificent arms and chest, and his six-pack abs that tapered into a vee that made her forget to be quiet. She really loved the way his muscles rippled as he walked...and how his erection thickened before her eyes.

"See what you do to me, Sandy?" he muttered, his arousal jutting out thick and long and proud, and she ached to have him inside her again.

Her mouth watered and body quivered as she watched him roll on the condom. He was taking care of protection before even getting under the covers. She liked that. A lot. It meant they didn't need to pause while in the throes of passion. "I love that you're coming in hot," she said with a smile, lifting the covers for him.

The air was cold, but his hands were warm on her ankles and in one swift move, he tugged her down the cushions until she was flat on her back again. She gasped. His take-charge, determined movements had her heart racing and desire flooding low in her belly in anticipation.

Archer crawled up her body, kissing and licking on his way to her mouth, where he plundered with a groan. His hands were skimming and caressing everywhere, spreading the heat that was simmering inside. Sandy traced his abs and would've gone lower, but he drew back, nudged her legs apart then entered in one thrust.

Her cry of pleasure mixed with his, echoing in the ocean breeze.

"You feel so good," he murmured, his voice raw with need.

Then he began to move, and she closed her eyes, riding the sensations. And when he slid a hand under her to spread her thighs and thrust in farther, she gasped and clutched his arms.

The moon was behind her, and it glinted off the silver in his hair and illuminated his face and the magnificence of his body. He dipped down and set his mouth on her throat as he pulled nearly all the way out, then drove back in, again and again, exactly opposite of the gentle rocking of the boat. Making her see stars—even when she closed her eyes.

"So damn good," he muttered, in that same, low, hoarse tone.

Heat flooded through her belly and settled between her legs where *he* felt so damn good, all big, and thick, and thrusting.

"Archer..."

He lifted up to stare down at her, his gaze unexpectedly open, sharing emotions with her, she knew the big, strong, alpha wouldn't normally reveal. Her throat tightened, incredibly humbled by the trust. By the special gift.

Needing to connect as much of her body to his as possible, she arched up, pressing her chest to his as she neared that blissful edge.

The angle afforded him to push even deeper inside. He made a raw, rough, sexy—almost possessive—sound deep in his chest as he captured her mouth, and their tongues mimicked the push and pull of their bodies.

Then he upped the pace, and it was all too much, and just right, and perfect. So perfect, she came with him buried deep inside, with barely any room for the cool ocean breeze to squeeze between them. Irrevocably connected, she trembled against him and around him, calling his name, and as he thrust deep and hard one last, delicious time, he followed her over the edge with her name falling from his lips.

***

Early the next morning before the sun even started to rise, Sandy arrived at the nest with Archer surprisingly rested, considering the amount of sleep they'd gotten last night. After spending three glorious hours on his boat, they'd headed back to his place for some more gloriousness and a little sleep.

Something had changed between them. Archer's touch had been different—still hot and incredible—but more grounded, sure, focused.

Like now. He stood by the coffee maker, waiting for it to brew, and slid his hands on her hips and drew her close, his gaze warm and determined. It was as if he knew what he wanted—*her*—and intended to get it.

And she was all right with that.

"Sorry to make you get up so early," he said, kissing her cheek.

She set her hands on his shoulders and smiled. "Don't be. I'm good."

It was the truth. She was satisfied and content, and figured that went a long way to contributing to feeling well-rested and energized. Or it could be the adrenaline rushing through her body because they were meeting up with the others to prepare to head to New York City in less than an hour.

"Yes, you are." He grinned, brushing her mouth with his. "Very good." Then he was pulling her in close and kissing her fully with just the right amount of heat that promised more later.

"Why don't you kiss me like that in the morning, Matteo?" Bella's voice drifted through the room, reminding her where they were. "Oh, that's right, you do."

Sandy was smiling as she drew back to meet Archer's gaze. "They found us."

"So it would seem." He returned her grin but didn't release her.

"Nah. Carry on," Bella said, pulling mugs out of the cupboard behind Archer. "I came in because I smelled coffee."

Laughing, she pulled out of Archer's arms, and once they all grabbed coffee, they headed to the sanctuary where TJ sat with his feet on the console while tapping the keyboard on his lap.

"Good. You're all here," he said, stopping to sit up and set his keyboard on the console. "I was just about to send up the bat signal."

Archer and Matteo snorted.

"Wrong comic book universe, TJ," Bella said, sitting down in her chair without spilling a drop of

193

coffee. "We're more Marvel than DC, but anyway, carry on."

"What have you got?" Archer asked, moving to stand in the middle of the room, his gaze bouncing from monitor to monitor.

"Actually, a few things," TJ said, his gaze serious. "I found something while you four were out...ah...sleeping." He tapped his keyboard several times and video appeared on one of the monitors near Bella. "I scoured the feed in Midtown, found several garages that stored carts, some kept logs of licenses, and bingo—I tracked down the cart and garage where Rodrigo stored his, then I found...well...this..."

The feed showed a large, white, supply truck backing up and Rodrigo unloading his cart, then pausing to inspect something at eye level, near the license. He removed the object, dropped it into his other hand, and frowned. A second later, the truck driver walked up to him, pulled out a gun with a silencer and shot him. Then quickly loaded Rodrigo's body into the back of the truck.

Sandy inhaled, and Archer slipped his arm around her shoulders and squeezed. Now they knew for sure that the guy hadn't been involved voluntarily. She blinked back the tears in her eyes and swallowed to clear her burning throat. "What was it he found?"

"A camera," TJ replied.

Archer muttered a curse. "They used his cart to survey the Reserve and DHS headquarters. The probably didn't like you taking photos, so they used the city's cameras to figure out your identity, and suspected you were going to interfere."

"And I was easier to track down than you," she said.

Archer nodded.

Matteo blew out a breath. "Rodrigo's roommate said he'd been given an unusual opportunity amongst the vendors to set up at a great spot. They must've manipulated things so Rodrigo was allowed to set up near your job as extra eyes to be sure you entered the building."

She frowned. "Wouldn't the mole just tell them? And why Rodrigo? Why not just put the camera on whatever vendor is usually there?"

"Because you established a rapport with him." Archer's face was grim. "And like Matteo said, those bastards like to manipulate things."

Bella set her empty mug on the console and waved at the monitors. "And mole or not, this kind of an outfit would use the camera on the cart as backup," Bella said. "I would."

Her chest tightened again as she watched the feed replay poor Rodrigo's murder. She stiffened. "Wait...I thought I saw..." Was her mind playing tricks? She moved away from Archer to step closer to the monitor. "TJ, zoom in on the truck driver." The guy was pretty good at keeping his face averted, but there was a small second when she'd gotten a glimpse of his reflection... "There. Pause it there."

"Son-of-a-bitch," Archer grumbled.

Matteo drew closer. "Is that Jimmy?"

"No way." Bella sat up, eyeing the screen.

Sandy shook her head. "Can't be. For two reasons. One, this guy is left-handed. He shot with his left hand, pulled keys out of his left pocket, whereas Jimmy was holding a pen in his right hand and reaching for his desk phone with his right hand, too, on the feed you have of him at the Reserve."

"Wow, good catch, Sherlock." TJ grinned.

Archer nodded. "And the second?"

She pointed to the feed. "The real Jimmy was tied up at headquarters in Brooklyn at that time."

"She's right." Bella waved at the monitor. "That was five minutes before Matteo and TJ left to go to the Reserve, and I headed out to extract the two of you near DHS." The woman shrugged. "Jimmy had been safe...well...safe might be the wrong word...but he was soundly in our custody at that time."

She watched Archer, wondering what was going on behind his intense gaze.

He stood staring at the monitor, arms folded across his chest, gaze narrowed. "They needed Jimmy as an *in* at the Reserve," he said. "Killed him when he'd outlived his usefulness and replaced him with one of their own—as they'd always intended—so they'd have someone inside." He nodded as if to himself. "They probably had people working inside the Munich museum, too."

Matteo moved to stand next to Archer, adopting a similar pose. "The reason they've been so hard to identify is because they have plastic surgery done to change their features for each job."

"And why there were several years between their bombings." Archer rubbed his jaw. "Took time to

196

research their target, select a new identity, have the surgery and recuperate before carrying out the job."

TJ whistled. "A deranged Mission Impossible fan."

"And they always chose to assume the identity of one of the workers with a similar height and build." Bella tapped a finger off her chin. "Genius."

Sandy was inclined to agree, and having a genius masterminding the bombing of the Federal Reserve did not give her the warm and fuzzies.

"TJ, run a search for Jimmy since his death," Archer said. "Maybe we'll get a location on the imposter."

The hacker swiveled his chair around toward the monitors, hands raised above the keyboard then stilled. "Found him."

"Dude, you're good, but..." Bella shook her head, brow raised.

TJ snickered. "True. Thanks, but I didn't need to look because he's right there." He pointed to the live feed at the Reserve. "He's sitting at Jimmy's desk right now."

"Shit," Matteo muttered.

Archer turned to Bella. "Get the chopper ready. We're heading to New York now."

"Roger that," the woman said, whipping out her phone. "I'll make a few calls. I can land us on top of a building three blocks south. The owner has a helipad for schmoozing bigwigs, and he owes me."

Matteo's head snapped in his wife's direction. "What owner? And why does he owe you?"

"Aww...you're jealous. That's sweet." Bella patted her husband's frowning face. "But don't be.

197

It was just business. I stopped a disgruntled client from chopping off his head and dropping it in the Hudson a few years ago."

Sandy would've laughed at the absurd story, only she suspected it was true.

"Three blocks south is good," Archer stated. "Don't want to get too close and tip our hand." He turned to her. "I need you to come and use a drone to listen for the boss's voice. You know what he sounds like now, and I trust you to pick it out again if you hear it."

She nodded, warmth spreading through her at his confidence in her. No way would she let that man down. "Do you want me to contact DHS to have them operate the drone?"

He blew out a breath and shook his head. "Not until they find the mole."

She nodded again.

"Want me to go, so I can operate it?" TJ asked.

It was better to have her hands free while listening so she could take notes, but it wasn't necessary.

"No," Archer said. "I need you to stay here and keep an eye on all the feeds, update us on any movement. Watch the Jimmy imposter and let us know when and where you see Mr. Clean, because I'm sure he's there, too."

"Roger that." TJ made a finger gun and pretended to shoot it at Archer. "I have the perfect drone for you, Sandy. It's smaller and can travel longer distances. I'll go get it."

If it was smaller than the one Bella had used last night, she hoped it was heavy enough to sustain the wind, since she was going to have to operate it between buildings. She also hoped no one would detect it out their window.

Archer, Bella, and Matteo also disappeared to change into their Federal Reserve Police uniforms Archer had acquired during his visit the other day. Sandy couldn't help but feel it was also a great disguise for Mr. Clean and the boss, since they already knew the Jimmy imposter worked at a desk and wore a suit.

She glanced down at her attire. Today she wore another sweater, this one in light blue, simple tan pants and comfortable tan flats. It would have to do.

"I'm back and I'm bearing gifts," TJ said, waltzing in with two metal suitcases in his hands just after the others returned. "Come get your coms on."

Sandy walked over with Bella and Matteo and listened as TJ explained how to operate the wrist watch-looking communicators they all strapped to their wrists. Archer strapped his com on, too, even though he was on the phone with Silas to update the man and make sure they had no trouble getting past Federal Reserve Police.

When TJ finished, Sandy shoved an earwig in her ear and reached for the drone, but Archer appeared by her side, and grabbed the suitcase off the table first. No longer talking on the phone, he used his free hand to shove in his earwig.

Damn...the man looked good in any uniform. This one was dark blue, almost black, and resembled a regular police uniform, complete with cap. He looked good enough to eat, but she kept that to herself. They had bad guys to bring to justice.

"I've got it," he said, turning to face her, hesitation and concern clouding his gaze, and for a moment she was afraid he was going to change his mind and order her to stay behind with TJ. But he lifted his chin and the hesitation drained away. "I don't want you to leave the rooftop we land on, okay?"

She reached up to cup his face. "Okay. I'll be fine. Don't worry about me. You stay safe and find these guys."

"Yeah. It's finally hunting time." Bella grinned, setting a foot on a nearby chair while she lifted her pants leg to strap a special holster to her ankle that housed both a knife and gun.

Guess the one on the woman's Federal Reserve Police-issued belt wasn't enough.

Apparently not, because Bella repeated the arming process on her other ankle. "I'm packing much lighter than I'm used to, but I doubt the Federal Reserve Police would appreciate me going in there fully loaded. As it is, I'm hoping they'll let me in like this."

Archer nodded. "They will. Silas is briefing the heads at the building now. No evacuation. Everything, unfortunately, has to appear normal if we're to have any luck grabbing this group." He set his gaze on each of them. "I'd rather be more prepared, but with the bomber boss' arrival last night, and the Jimmy imposter in that building right now, it's where we need to be, too. We'll have to wing it."

"No problem, sir," Matteo said. "SEALs taught us to adapt."

Archer nodded, a slight twitch to his lips. "That, they did." Then his attention turned to her, and he handed her a holstered Glock from out of thin air. "I know you're staying on that roof, but I don't want you going unarmed."

Once again, Sandy was touched by the show of faith the man had in her abilities. She knew he had a hard time accepting that she was capable of using a weapon and suspected it was because he was worried if she shot at someone, they'd shoot back. But it was part of her job, even if it was a small part, since most of the time her work was done behind a computer.

"Thanks," she told him, and went through the safety process of checking the pistol before attaching the holster and gun to her right ankle. It might not be her Glock, but she already felt better with the reassuring weight of the weapon on her leg. She was packing others, though. The hair sticks holding her bun in place. They were weapon gifts from Bella.

"Is there anything else you want me to do?" she asked, feeling like she wasn't contributing enough.

"Yeah." He stepped right into her personal space and cupped her face. "Stay safe."

She inhaled and blew out the breath, running her hands up his chest, fighting to keep her emotions at bay. "I will, if you will."

His jaw worked a time or two before he walked her backward two feet, until her back hit the wall and his mouth came down on hers for a fast, hot, desperate kiss, conveying all his worries and fears and hopes. Sandy returned the embrace, wishing it could last and that the incredible man holding her didn't have to go search out a mad bomber with a crazy IQ and no regard for life.

Archer broke the kiss, but continued to cup her face while he held her gaze. "We'll finish this later."

Drawing air into her lungs, she nodded. "Roger that."

A smile quirked his lips before he released her and stepped back, his SEAL in charge persona washing over him to turn her lover back into her boss.

Sandy straightened her shoulders and refused to allow her mind to worry about him or the team, or all the innocent people who could get hurt today if they failed.

Failure was not an option.

They knew about the Jimmy look-a-like, and to keep an eye out for Mr. Clean. She just wished they knew what the boss looked like. *And* if there was anyone else that was part of the crew.

With luck and TJ's drone, Sandy was determined to find the bomber so Archer could end this madness before it started.

CHAPTER SIXTEEN

Not far from the nest, they pulled in to the local airstrip—the same one where Archer had boarded a flight with Silas the other day, and where Bella had rented helicopters when needed for Knight Agency ops. The one she rented for them today was fueled up and ready to go, so she performed a quick maintenance check before proclaiming it flight ready.

Good. The sooner they got to the city, the better. He should've made everyone travel up last night when their target had escaped to the open ocean. It was obvious the bastard was headed for New York Harbor, since all the chatter around him had mentioned New York.

He clenched his hands into fists then splayed his fingers out wide before relaxing them. To be fair, at the time they hadn't known about the Jimmy imposter or they would've been up there as soon as they'd found out.

What was done, was done. It was a waste of time stressing over something that *should've* been and prudent to focus on what *could* be.

That held true in personal life as well as business, and considering the line between both was currently smudged, he chose to look forward, not backward, and turn that *could be* into *is now*.

After helping Sandy get seated in the back and buckled in, he climbed into the front passenger seat, needing to keep his mind sharp and in op mode. But damn, it'd been tough to leave her side. His desire to protect her was something he had trouble burying, and exactly what he intended to accomplish by the time they reached the city in forty-five minutes.

He brought to mind images and memories of that day in Munich and vowed to take this man and his team down for those people whose lives they cut short, and for the surviving families who were forced to live without their loved ones.

Today was for them.

And Rodrigo.

And to prevent any more innocent blood from spilling because of these madmen, especially so damn close to where his father and brother had died at the hands of a similar bastard.

By the time they'd touched down on the rooftop of the building owned by a businessman who owed Bella a favor, Archer's mindset was solid, adrenaline pumped, and he was ready to carry out the mission tasked to him by his buddy Silas, the head of Bone Frog Command at DHS. He knew the division was Silas' brainchild, and new, with the potential for other retired SEALs to have the opportunity to use their training to carry out missions for their country, just as he was doing today. Archer was not about to let any of them down, either.

Was there a lot at stake today?

Fuck, yeah.

Was he going to fail?

No fucking way.

As Bella powered down, Archer exited the chopper and opened the door for Sandy, not surprised to find her already unbuckled, with the drone suitcase in her hand. He helped her deboard and held onto her hand a few extra seconds as she stood in front of him, her gaze full of the same feelings he was letting her see in his eyes.

They had unfinished business. He would be fine, but he was damn glad she wasn't going with him. Knowing she was safer here than with him in the building with the bomb threat made it easier for him to leave her behind to do her job.

A second later, Bella and Matteo joined them from the other side of the chopper, signaling they were ready to roll. Archer released Sandy with one last squeeze before he turned on his heel and strode across the rooftop to where an older man in a fancy suit smiled and waved at them behind a large glass door.

As they neared, a burly man in a suit opened the door and stepped aside while they entered the building into one large, vacant room. It appeared to be a lounge area, with a gigantic TV screen behind a large bar, two walls of windows, and another with an elevator and a door he assumed led to the stairwell.

"Bella, my hero," the man crooned, grasping her upper arms while leaning in to kiss her on each cheek with a flourish. Archer felt Matteo stiffen next to him, but he had to give the man credit, he didn't lose his cool. "Always a pleasure to see you. And don't you look adorable in that uniform."

"Good to see you still have your head, Mr. Horvath." She winked, receiving a snort from their host. Smirking, she turned to them and made the introductions. "This is my husband, Matteo."

The man gasped and clasped Matteo's hand in both of his while he pumped it up and down. "It is an honor to meet the luckiest man in the world."

"Indeed...I am," Matteo said, efficiently slipping an arm around Bella, while removing his other hand from the man's grasp.

Well played, Archer thought, while thrusting his hand to their host. "Archer Malone," he said, shaking hands. "Thank you for allowing us to land, and for letting Sandy work from your rooftop." He nodded toward the far corner, where she was opening the drone case.

"But, of course," Mr. Horvath replied. "Any friend of Bella's is mine, too. I was just about to sit down for a brunch I'm hosting for several business acquaintances. You are all more than welcome to join."

"Thank you, but no," Bella said, setting a hand on the man's shoulder as she guided him to the elevator. "But if you could make sure Sandy has some water, I'd appreciate it. The sun is very direct this morning."

"Consider it done," their host said, sending a pointed look to the burly man, who immediately fished a bottle of water from behind the bar and rushed outside to hand it to Sandy.

Feeling better knowing she was here with hospitable people, Archer hit the down button on the elevator, eager to get where they needed to be. When it opened, they all piled in, including Mr. Horvath and the burly dude, and Archer was glad the elevator was huge, with an equally huge weight limit.

Their host got off four floors down and turned to them. "If you finish your business in time, we'll be having brunch until one, then putting on a huge spread for dinner at five. Feel free to stop in for one, or both."

"Thank you," Bella said, pressing the Close Door button and Lobby button, and holding them in.

Archer wasn't sure that express elevator trick would work in this building but hoped it would, since there were over fifty floors and they didn't have any more time to waste.

"Does he always put his hands on you?" Matteo asked his wife after the doors closed.

Archer leaned his back against the far wall and settled in to watch the floor show to kill time.

Still holding the buttons in, she turned to smile at her husband. "Does that really bother you?"

Matteo lifted a shoulder. "Depends."

"Oh?" A wicked gleam entered her gaze. "On what?"

He could sense his buddy stiffen up. "On where he touches you."

"Relax." She chuckled. "You know you're the only one I allow to touch me in the ways you're implying."

Matteo blew out a breath and his hard features eased into a grin. "Yeah, I know."

"Archer," Bella said, leaning toward Matteo, her hands still on the buttons as they descended past the twentieth floor. Apparently the express trick worked. "Just warning you I'm going to kiss my husband now and there might be some tongue…correction, there *better* be some tongue."

He chuckled and shook his head as Matteo gave his wife what she wanted—which, by the look of it—was no doubt what his buddy wanted, too. But because the angle appeared uncomfortable and he didn't want to watch, Archer stepped toward the control panel and pressed his thumbs to the buttons under her fingers.

"You can let go now and grab your husband, Bella," he told her, and a second later she nearly knocked him over in her haste to align her body to Matteo's without breaking the kiss.

Their eagerness and the way their passion morphed out of control reminded Archer of his connection with Sandy. A simple kiss could turn into a full-blown, throbbing need to lift her up and take her against the nearest wall or solid object in the space of a single heartbeat.

What really astounded him about Matteo was how the guy could work with his wife in this type of business, even though Bella was extremely capable of taking care of herself. Archer couldn't stand the thought of Sandy being in harm's way. Hell, even now, he hated leaving her side, despite the fact she was safe, and he was headed toward the danger.

"Sandy?" he said quietly. "Can you hear me?"

Their communications were set to open, which meant all five of them were connected.

"Yes," she immediately replied, a smile in her tone. "I can hear everything."

He snickered. "Doubt they care."

Her soft laugh sent goosebumps down his neck and chest. "Roger that."

It was the mark of a good team member when they followed protocol and didn't comment, despite the interesting things she'd definitely heard. Perhaps, given time, working with her permanently might be something Archer would come to terms with, but for now, he was glad it was Matteo's wife accompanying them to the Reserve and not Sandy.

To his amazement, Bella and Matteo drew apart without needing him to prompt them, which he was about to do since they just passed the fifth floor. When they reached the lobby and the doors opened, the three of them were back into agent mode and remained that way during their three-block trek to the employee entrance of the Federal Reserve.

Whatever it was Silas had told their boss must've been good, because after flashing their credentials, they were immediately ushered inside, but went through the security process like the other employees.

Archer couldn't fault them for that.

Once they were through, they each headed to their pre-determined locations. Bella went upstairs to the fifth floor to observe the Jimmy imposter, Matteo checked in with the head of security, and Archer asked to be taken downstairs to check on the gold, even though TJ had eyes on it.

Each undertaking took some time, especially his, because it required several security protocols.

"Jimmy-*point-one* is chillin' at his desk," Bella informed. "TJ, can you hear me?"

"Loud and clear," came the hacker's quick reply. "I've been listening but remained quiet to keep chatter down."

Archer gave TJ credit as well, for remaining silent the whole time so far.

"Can you see what Jimmy *Imp* is doing on his computer?" Bella asked. "The monitor is facing the wall, so unless I walk in and stand behind him, I can't tell."

The woman was stationed in a large break room across the hall diagonally from the imposter's office.

"That's a big ten-four," TJ replied. "The Imp is playing solitaire."

Archer frowned but said nothing since he was standing near two FRPs, who guarded the elevator that led to the gold. The men were unaware of his duty, they only knew he was waiting for a supervisor to take him downstairs.

"Solitaire? Seriously?" Bella grumbled. "Okay, I'll keep an eye on him."

"Me, too," TJ said. "And no Mr. Clean sightings yet, either."

"He's here somewhere," Matteo joined the chat.

"Keeping my eyes, peeled," TJ said. "Sandy, how's the drone treating you?"

"Good. I love it," she said. "Nice design. So far, though, I haven't heard anything pertaining to the mission. Or the voice from last night."

Damn.

Archer kept his face dialed to expressionless but was getting antsy. Something was definitely going down today with the Jimmy imposter filling in here. And with the Rodrigo murder investigation still ongoing, it would force any normal person to want to leave the city as soon as possible.

Of course, there wasn't anything normal about this bastard. Which remained true when he finally got the tour of downstairs and found nothing amiss. Each cell represented a country and held stacks of gold bars. There weren't any vending machines, or garbage cans, or filing cabinets, or anything at all in that area but concrete, steel, and gold.

For someone who supposedly wanted to rob or blow up the gold, the guy wasn't acting like it.

"Negatory on downstairs," he said after returning to the lobby. "Nothing odd."

"Mr. Clean sighting heading down hall on ninth floor," TJ reported. "Wearing FRP uniform as well. He removed the cap, and my computer spotted the tattoo."

"On it," Bella stated. "I'm closest."

Archer entered the nearest stairwell and took them two at a time on his sprint up to the fifth floor to take over watching the imposter, who was the only one in the two-man office today. "We need him alive, Bella. We need answers."

"Roger that," she said. "TJ, what room?"

"Was in 908, but is now entering men's room," TJ replied. "Of which I have eyes on, thanks to Archer/Matteo recon earlier this week."

Placing cameras in bathrooms fell far down on Archer's list of fun things to do. He entered the fifth floor and walked down the hall to resume Bella's post near a water cooler.

"Entering," Bella said, underlying excitement in her tone. "Excuse me, sir. We need to talk."

A click sounded through the comm link.

"She just locked the door." TJ chuckled. "Sorry," he whispered.

Archer clenched his jaw. He hated waiting. And not having eyes on.

"Hey...dude...what the?" Shock lifted Bella's tone a second before a scuffle sounded, followed by a thud. "Ah...TJ, you get that?"

A sigh rustled through the comms. "Yeah...that was crazy."

"You okay, Bella?" Matteo asked.

"Yes," she replied. "But Mr. Clean is now Mr. Dead."

Shit.

Archer barely swallowed that one down. "What happened?"

"It wasn't my fault," Bella insisted.

This time Archer didn't bother to hold back his snort. That statement and Bella didn't fit.

"It's true," TJ said. "The guy pulled a pill out of his pocket then swallowed it like he was in the cold war era and keeled over dead."

"I tried to stop him, but he was too far away." Bella sighed. "Checking his pockets now."

Archer waited for what felt like years before she continued.

"Nothing, except a cylindrical metal keychain that doesn't give me the warm and fuzzies," she said. "He doesn't have a wallet or even any loose change. TJ, get a still shot of this keychain and run it."

"Done...shit," the hacker muttered. "It's a bomb."

"Bella, be careful, don't jumble it," Matteo said, concern tight in his voice. "I'm on my way up."

Archer's pulse raced almost as fast as his mind. If one of them had a bomb, so could the other. He strode across the break room. It was time to get answers.

"Why do I have the feeling the fake Jimmy has one, too?" Sandy asked, her voice full of concern.

"I'm heading there to check now," Archer said, halting by the door as a group of people walked in, blocking his exit. "Excuse me," he said, pushing his way through in time to see the imposter take a cylindrical keychain out of his pocket and set it in the top drawer of his desk before he stood.

With a crowd in the break room and several people in the hall, Archer decided not to pull his gun. Instead, he entered the office without a sound, snuck up behind the imposter, and in a swift move, grabbed the man by the back of the head and slammed his face straight down into the other desk. Twice.

For Rodrigo.

Then he cuffed the groaning, bleeding man before the guy's mind had a chance to register what had happened.

"Damn...nice moves, Archer," TJ said.

He searched the dazed man's pockets, finding a lone pill, Jimmy's ID badge, no wallet, or loose change like Mr. Clean, and a gun with a silencer. Archer wondered how the guy had gotten it past security.

Didn't matter. It was in Archer's possession now. And ballistics would most likely match it to Rodrigo's wounds. With extra care, he opened the top drawer of Jimmy's desk and spotted the keychain. "TJ, what did you dig up about these bombs?"

"Consulting someone now," the hacker said.

Archer had come across something similar once, during an op in Bangladesh. "Matteo, you upstairs with Bella? That keychain look familiar to you?"

"Yes, and yes," his buddy said. "Bangladesh."

He blew out a breath. "Are your dots connected?" There were three tiny dots. Two on the stationary top portion and one on the middle that held a highly dangerous liquid explosive, but not enough to blow up half the building.

Were there more? What exactly was this group up to?

"No. They're not connected," Matteo said. "We must've caught him before he'd had the chance to arm it."

Archer exhaled and nodded. "Good. Unfortunately, this one is." And he knew the imposter would lie if asked, so they weren't going that route.

In Bangladesh, a twist to the right deactivated the bomb, and to the left detonated it, if they did nothing, it would detonate by remote.

"Barb worked several bomb details," Sandy said. "I can call her."

He shook his head as if she could see him. "No. Thanks. I'd rather not involve DHS, if we can help it. Sorry."

A sigh rustled through the comm. "I understand."

Matteo walked into the room, glanced at the unconscious, bleeding man slumped against the wall, and raised a brow. Archer shrugged.

"But if you're at all unsure we need to call her," Sandy said. "Or call someone."

"I'm ninety percent sure it's left to deactivate and right to detonate." He contemplated taking the keychain to the water and tossing it in, but the walk was too far and he had no idea what, if anything, might set it off on the way. "What about you, Matteo?"

"Same," his buddy replied.

"That's not a hundred, Archer." Concern deepened Sandy's tone.

"But Jameson is," TJ said, talking about his boss and Archer's very capable, lethal, knowledgeable buddy. "I sent him the video and he said turn to the left."

If Jameson Knight told him to the left, then it was to the left. So Archer reached into the draw for the bomb, sent up a silent prayer just in case, and twisted it to the left. "Done."

He exhaled and slumped against the desk.

"Well, now...all things considered, this is a nice consolation prize." A familiar voice sounded in the background of someone's com and stopped Archer's heart.

He stiffened, and his whole body felt the utter stillness, right down to his skipped heartbeat.

It was *him*.

The voice from Munich. The bomber.

Knowing he hadn't heard it in real time, Archer glanced across the room at Matteo to see who was near the man, eager to lay eyes on the goddamn bomber after all these years. But the area was vacant, and no one was behind him in the hallway. Matteo met his gaze and shook his head.

Shit.

The boss was not on their floor.

"I just heard the dude's voice," TJ said.

"Bella? You got eyes on him?" he asked. The target must be upstairs with her.

"I'm making my way down to you guys," she said over the com. "I heard him, too."

Wait…if he wasn't with Bella either…

Archer's heart dropped to his knees.

Then it meant…

"Ms. Vickers, isn't it?" the bomber's voice trickled through the coms again. "So nice to meet you in person."

CHAPTER SEVENTEEN

Dammit.

She was supposed to be safe on that building. Away from that damn madman and any harm he may inflict. Instead, she was a sitting duck.

Bella entered the room, motioning with a thumbs up that the wall of Federal Reserve Police gathering outside the door were waiting for him to give them instructions.

Archer set the keychain on the desk, scrubbed a hand over his face and contemplated punching the wall, until he heard the imposter snicker.

"I take it you've heard from the boss." The guy snickered again.

Archer lunged forward with his fist above his head and brought it down hard across the asshole's cheekbone.

Much more satisfying than hitting a wall.

He flexed his throbbing hand, embracing the pain, letting it heat his blood that had run cold only moments before. "Sandy, it'll be okay. I'm coming to get you."

"Okay," she whispered.

"Ah, isn't that sweet," the bastard said.

Fuck.

His gaze shot to Matteo, then Bella. The guy was listening in. He'd been listening the whole damn time.

"So, here's how this is going to go down," the bastard said, his voice louder than before, which meant...he was closer to Sandy. "You are going to put both of my bombs back *and* activate them or your precious Sandy just might trip and fall off this building. She was operating that drone awfully close to the edge."

That son-of-bitch. If he so much as...

Rage shook through Archer so fierce his teeth rattled. But a level head was needed to deal with this madman. "Two bombs?" he asked instead of begging for Sandy's life.

Even though he'd gladly do it...it would be fruitless. Archer knew the man was going to kill her no matter what he did, so he just had to play along to keep her alive long enough for him to rescue her. First thing he needed to do was find out if the devices on their wrists were hacked or if it was just the com lines.

"Yes, two," the guy said. "Why?"

Christ, he couldn't believe he was about to answer him. "Because by my estimate, there aren't enough explosives here to bring down the whole building."

His stomach rolled at having said that out loud.

"Correct. But who says I want to bring it all down?"

What the fuck was he up to?

"Just enough to cause chaos while you rob the place?" Sandy asked.

Archer's chest tightened, and he silently willed her not to speak to the man.

"Not a bad idea, if I had wanted to rob it."

Matteo frowned and shook his head.

Bella had a lethal gleam in her eyes, and Archer was more than happy to sic the former terrorist hunter on the madman

"So, you don't want to rob it or completely destroy it," he said, hoping the man would fill in the blanks.

"Correct," the bastard repeated, but didn't elaborate.

"You want to blow it up enough to cause carnage and expose the vault so the public could reach the gold to loot it and create chaos," Sandy said.

Jesus...

The visual her words painted made Archer nauseous.

"Ah, you are a smart cookie, Ms. Vickers. I think I'm going to enjoy our time together."

Archer's jaw and neck were stiff, and a churning heat flooded his stomach. Everything inside Archer banded together and filled with a singular purpose...to save Sandy from this madman.

The strap on his wrist vibrated, reminding him of the communicator's other abilities. Like video feed he was getting.

Good girl, Sandy.

His pulse kicked up as he caught a glimpse of the bomber whose voice had tormented Archer for years. Sandy managed to activate the feature and angle her wrist enough to capture the target on video.

Even though they had to assume the man's face wasn't his original, Archer was hopeful they'd get some kind of ID.

"All right, enough chit chat," the target said. "There's no need to cut the power in the building, just put my bombs back in play, and remember, I'll be watching."

As carefully as he could, Archer sent a text message to TJ, asking about having a location on Sandy.

STILL ON HORVATH'S BUILDING.

Then he asked TJ to sever the video feed in the FRB long enough for them to get outside.

No way were they setting any damn bombs for the bastard.

When TJ told them they were good to go, Archer shoved the keychain from the desk into his pocket. "You do have the other one, right, Bella?" he asked.

She nodded and patted her hip pocket. "Yes."

He glanced at the unconscious man now sporting a black eye. They couldn't take him, he'd slow them down. Nor could he just leave the guy...

Or could he?

He had TJ send the police and the officer in charge at the Federal Reserve the feed of Rodrigo's murder while Archer pulled the imposter's gun from his pocket and set it on the desk. He explained why his prints were on the gun to the officer in charge and asked him to keep the imposter in custody until the police arrived.

Then they rushed out of the building and ran for Horvath's building. Archer hoped the bomber couldn't hear their conversation anymore. TJ insisted his wrist comms were secure and that their target was using something like his drone to eavesdrop.

In case it was true, Archer sent Sandy a quick text telling her he was coming.

When they got to the building, it felt like it took the express elevator an hour instead of the actual time of five minutes to climb the fifty stories to the top floor. But when they arrived, guns drawn, the floor was empty except for Horvath and his bodyguard, both bleeding on the floor. The owner only had a broken nose, the other man was bleeding from a hole in his shoulder.

Matteo hurried to the men, pulling out his phone. "I'm calling for help now. Just keep pressure on the wound."

Archer rushed outside, Bella on his heels, but there was no Sandy. No bomber. No chopper.

They were too late.

His insides felt as if they'd folded in on themselves. And despite being outside, he couldn't get any air into his lungs. He called TJ and managed to talk. "Tell me you're tracking her."

"I'm tracking her."

Thank Christ.

Archer finally sucked air into his lungs. "Where?"

The man had a helicopter. He could get anywhere with it.

"Over the East River. Looks like they're landing on a boat. Check on your wrist comm," he said. "I sent the tracking to all your comms."

He walked back inside and headed to where Matteo knelt, still helping the bodyguard and Bella's friend.

"Mr. Horvath, you need to find some new friends," Bella said, grabbing some ice from behind the bar, and wrapping it in a napkin before returning to hold it on his nose.

"I wish you had been here." He shuddered. "I don't understand. I've known Roger for over twenty years. What would make him do such a thing?"

"What, exactly, did he do?" Bella asked quietly.

"We came up here for something a little stronger to drink than the champagne from brunch. He said he wanted to enjoy the view. He and his bodyguard shot up my TV. And then he saw your lady friend, and I'm sorry, but he took her and your helicopter."

Bella set a hand on the man's shoulder. "Was he piloting?"

"No. His bodyguard flew it."

Archer stared down at the man. "Was there anyone else?"

"No."

Good. "Do you have any idea where he might take her?"

"Well, maybe his super yacht, The Commandant." The man removed the ice from his nose and shrugged. "He usually likes to cruise out to sea from the East River."

"No other real estate? Penthouse? Apartment?" Archer asked.

"No, he always stays here on my property." Horvath shook his head again. "This just doesn't make sense. Roger doesn't even like guns."

"I'm sorry," Bella said, patting his hand. "But I'm afraid that wasn't your friend. It was an imposter, who had surgery to look like someone whose identity he'd assumed."

Horvath frowned. "That wasn't Roger?"

"No." She shook her head. "I'm sorry, but it's likely the real Roger—your friend—is dead."

His eyes widened on an inhale. "Oh."

Twenty minutes later, Archer and his team were on the East River, making their way to their two objectives.

Rescue Sandy and take out the target.

Archer knew his team, their strengths and weaknesses and had no trouble delegating duties. Bella was going to hunt down and take out the target. He was going to find Sandy and get her off the ship before the fireworks started. Matteo was their EXFIL.

Sandy's signal was still coming in strong, and was, indeed, from The Commandant, still in port. TJ was already dialed into whatever the guy had dialed into.

And Archer was ready…he was ready for this to be over and Sandy to be safe. Taking a chance their target wouldn't find out, he sent Sandy one last text.

HANG TIGHT. I'M COMING TO GET YOU. BE READY.

Since they weren't fortunate enough to have the cover of darkness, Archer and Bella decided to board from the water and rope climb onto the large yacht. They followed Sandy's signal, still coming in strong. She was sitting at a table in the galley.

Hands and feet zip tied. Bruise on her right cheekbone.

Inhaling, he clenched his jaw. He was going to fucking kill whoever had touched her.

The ship was eerily empty of crew, and yet the engines kicked on and the yacht headed away from port. He signaled for Bella to go below deck, and he stayed up top to recon the heat sources showing up on their watches. Using blades, he took out three at the bow, and she sliced through three on the deck below. Then she went to the helm and he entered the galley and rushed to Sandy.

"You okay?" he asked quietly, while quickly cutting through her restraints and pulling her to her feet for a quick hug.

"Yes." She nodded. "But hurry, he was really mad when no bombs detonated."

"Yes, Archer, please do hurry," the bastard said from the doorway, gun in hand, but pointed to the deck. "Now that you're here, I can at least amuse myself by killing her in front of you. Slowly."

He pushed Sandy behind him to shield her with his body. "Not gonna happen." He felt Sandy remove one of the guns behind his back, but he knew that wasn't needed either.

Bella was on the loose.

The woman *was* a weapon, so he was letting her do her thing. It would be swift and lethal. All he had to do was keep the man distracted, and Sandy safe, while she cleared the rest of the yacht.

The target waved his gun and smirked and didn't seem to realize they were slowing down, because Bella, no doubt, took out the pilot. "My old friend

Walter says different. You only postponed the inevitable today. This city knows that the second time is much worse. I only used a handful of people. Think what I can do with a dozen or two loyalists."

His stomach roiled at the thought.

"Who were you blackmailing at DHS?" Sandy asked from behind his back.

The bastard chuckled. "Ah, you are smart. You guessed correctly. Poor...Amy. Women are such easy victims. They'd do anything to keep their child from having an unfortunate accident on her way home from school."

He felt Sandy's gasp but watched the target's mouth drop open while Bella stuck a blade in his back.

"You should never underestimate a woman," she said, knocking the gun from the man before plunging her other knife into the right side of his chest. "Especially a Banshee." Then she removed her blades, wiping them off on the guy's shoulders before sheathing them at her sides. When she stood back, he dropped to his knees, face still stuck in that shocked expression as he slowly bled out.

Archer glanced at his wrist communicator to check for any other signs of life on the yacht, but only saw their three. Certain it was safe, he tugged Sandy past the dead bastard to the stern, which was free from bodies, then pulled her into his arms and just held her while she started to shake.

"It's okay," he murmured against her temple, so damn glad to hold her safely in his arms.

She slid her arms around him and held him just as tight. "God...I thought he was going to shoot you. If Bella hadn't..."

"Shh..." He ran a hand up and down her back. "I knew she was there."

She nodded, then drew back. "And I knew you'd come for me."

"Always," he said, kissing her temple, her nose, then very lightly on her bruised cheek. "Did he hit you?"

"No." She shook her head. "It was his bodyguard. He didn't take too kindly to my knee to his crotch."

"Oorah," Bella, the former Marine, called from behind. "I'm going to take us in now."

"Is Matteo okay?" Sandy asked, concern darkening her gaze.

Archer nodded. "Yes. He stayed back. He was our EXFIL if we needed it." He pulled her in close, buried his face in her neck, and breathed.

Christ. It was the first real breath he'd taken since hearing that bastard's voice through the com line. "When I heard him in your link..."

Her arms slid around to his chest and she drew back to look at him. "I'm fine. No...I'm better than fine, when I'm with you."

"I'm glad to hear you say that, Sandy, because I don't want to stop seeing you. I'm willing to drive in whenever you'll have me. And I hope you'll come to the shore and stay however long you want."

She smiled up at him. "I'd like all of it. And anything I can have from you. Anything I can get. Whatever you're willing to give."

"How about all of me?" He cupped her face. "Because you already do."

Her eyes were full of a tenderness that caught at his heart, melting thru each layer of steel he'd erected around it after losing first his unborn child, then his father and his brother. With her in his life, his chest felt lighter, unrestricted, free from barriers...free to feel, and staring into her open, fathomless gaze, he felt the one emotion that had eluded him for decades...hope.

EPILOGUE

One year later…

If someone would've told Archer a year ago, he'd be enjoying retirement from the teams and happily married to his former froglet's mother, he would've accused them of being drunk.

But he was enjoying being stateside and spending his time with the woman he loved instead of hunkered down in some third world country with his SEAL brothers. As for marrying Sandy? Best damn day of his life was seven months ago, on a warm September Saturday, when Brian walked his gorgeous mother down the beach behind their home and allowed him the privilege to pledge his heart to the woman he loved with everything inside him.

They'd united their lives together in front of family and friends. Gus, his mother—Jameson had been his best man, and Barb had been Sandy's maid of honor…the two seemed to hit it off pretty well, although, his buddy would never give anything away. Bella and Matteo stood up with them too, and, Silas and his family were there. The little baby had been a big hit with his mother. The day had been perfect. The only thing that would've made it better would've been to have his father and brother there to celebrate with him.

He gained a wife, and he'd like to think a son, that day. And it was nice to have guests at the old homestead, laughing and enjoying the place like his father had wanted. It felt warm and like a home again. Even his mother visited him now at least once a month, and Archer attributed all of it to the woman walking by his side now, holding his hand, warmth and encouragement in her eyes.

"Hard to believe it was a year ago, right here on this spot, one of my favorites in all of New York, because of you." She smiled up at him. "You kissed me to keep up our ruse right on this very corner. Remember?"

Remember?

"How could I forget?" He slid his arms around Sandy's waist and turned them until his back was against the building...just as it had been on the first day of their assignment together. "You rocked my world that day."

Everything about that assignment had been crazy. A bald guy with an eye tattoo on the back of his head. Threats to her. Threats to the Reserve. Ghosts from the past. Plastic surgeries done off the books. TJ had been able to track down the actual identity of the bomber they had been forced to call Roger, who was actually William Fennel.

Raised by an abusive mother, Willy grew up in a criminal environment but with a high IQ. He started as a hacker-for-hire, eventually moving up to bomber-for-hire. Then he kept expanding, and started changing his identities, always choosing someone rich with similar body-types and continued to amass his wealth on top of what terror organizations began to pay him, until he became a global threat.

Willy'd had an aptitude for electronics and computers, and managed to hack into whatever he wanted. Archer was just lucky the man hadn't known about the wrist communicators. And luckily the guy hadn't had a large crew...or more bombs. Matteo had watched over them while he and Bella had gone after Willy/Roger. Later, they'd turned them over to Silas, who'd also confirmed that the life of the seven-year-old daughter of Amy Spencer, the fourteenth-floor receptionist, had been threatened. DHS had found no other moles and he was inclined to believe it had been just the desperate mother.

"Roger that," she said leaning against him. "There was nothing fake about the way I felt then or now, Archer. I love you."

He skimmed his fingers along her jawline, completely drawn in and owned by this woman. "I love you, too."

She pressed feather-light kisses to his lips...and those where the ones that reset his soul.

"Ready?" she asked quietly.

He swallowed past a dry throat and straightened from the wall. "Yes." And together they walked hand-in-hand, silently closer to the one place in New York City he'd avoided for over a decade.

The memorial.

It'd always been too difficult. His heart hadn't been ready. He'd had the shattered pieces buried underneath layers of indifference, anger, denial...all things that held him back from really opening up and giving everything to the woman who irrevocably gave him her all. Archer wanted to reciprocate...to give her what she deserved—all of him. He'd do anything for her. But he also knew he was doing this for him, too.

He was ready. Ready to stand at the last place his father and brother had been alive. Ready to read their names on the wall. Ready to find a way to move forward.

The closer they got, the harder it was to drag air into his lungs. Sandy squeezed his hand but waited with him every time he stopped. Finally, though...finally he made it all the way and stood there staring at the beautiful, peaceful place.

He touched the wall, ran his finger over their names, and he felt as if a light breeze blew through him, removing some of the darkness he hadn't realized he still harbored. Sandy never left his side. Never offered empty words, just offered her touch, and her understanding, for she, too, ran her finger over a name—Rhonda Vickers—and a tear escaped down her cheek.

"My mother-in-law," she said quietly. "She was a secretary for an insurance company. I was on the phone with her, talking about Brian's preschool photos when the first plane hit." She swallowed. "I stayed on the phone with her until the line went dead."

Her resilience never ceased to amaze Archer. She'd been through so much, taken so many hits, and yet, she kept looking forward. God, he loved her.

Bending down, he kissed her softly, and stood there enjoying the connection while the light breeze blew…and her phone rang.

Anticipation lit her face when she glanced at the caller ID. "Hello? Yes, this is she." Her blue eyes held his and she inhaled and swallowed. "Okay, I will. Thank you."

"Good news?" He raised a brow, trying to figure out what was going on in her head, because she had a knowing look in her eyes that was driving him wild.

"Depends." She bit her lower lip while holding his gaze.

Had she applied for another job at DHS? For the past three months she'd strictly worked for the Knight Agency in AC as an analyst when needed, and he helped them out too, when needed. They were both semi-retired and enjoying life.

So, was she getting bored?

He cleared his throat. "Depends on what?"

"On whether you're okay with being a daddy," she said, the last part coming out a little soft as she seemed to hold her breath.

His breath was gone. It'd disappeared with his ability to think. "A dad?" He blinked when she nodded. "You're pregnant?" She nodded again.

He was going to be a father…

A surge of happiness burst through him. "Hooyah!" He picked her up and twirled her around into a big hug. "Are you okay?" He halted and set her feet gently on the ground. "I didn't make you sick, did I?"

She chuckled. "No, that's around the corner, though." A grimace wrinkled her face. "But, I'm sure you'll be great at back rubs."

"You already know I am." He set his forehead to hers and ran his hands down her arms. "Are you okay with this? I know we're not in our twenties, but I think we still have a lot to offer."

"Absolutely." She grabbed his hand and set his palm on her still flat belly. "You are going to make a wonderful father. This baby is already so very blessed."

He was the one who was blessed.

Blessed the day this mother of a SEAL walked into his life and loved a bonefrog bum like him.

Dear Readers,

If you enjoyed SEAL IN CHARGE, please consider leaving a review. Thank you.

The Silver Series stories continue in SEAL in a Storm by KaLyn Cooper with Navy SEAL commander Dex Carson.

And if you enjoyed meeting Matteo and Bella from the Knight Agency, you can read their stories and others, in my ***Dangerous Curves Series***!

Thanks for reading,

~Donna

SILVER SEALS

SEAL *Strong* - Cat Johnson

SEAL *Love's Legacy* - Sharon Hamilton

SEAL *Together* - Maryann Jordan

SEAL *of Fortune* - Becky McGraw – *POSTPONED DUE TO ILLNESS*

SEAL *in Charge* - Donna Michaels

SEAL *in a Storm* - KaLyn Cooper

SEAL *Forever* - Kris Michaels

SEAL *Out of Water* - Abbie Zanders

Sign, SEAL *and Deliver* - Geri Foster

SEAL *Hard* - J.m. Madden

SEAL *Undercover* - Desiree Holt

SEAL *for Hire* - Trish Loye

SEAL *at Sunrise* - Caitlyn O'Leary

facebook.com/SilverSEALSeries

SilverSEALs.com

Don't miss Donna Michaels'

~Dangerous Curves Series~

Knight's SEAL

LOCKE and Load

A DAYE with a SEAL

Cowboy LAWE

Connected to Dangerous Curves:

Elite Protector (Elle James' Brotherhood Protectors)

Grinch REAPER (Sleeper SEALs Series)

SEAL in Charge (Silver SEALs Series)

Also by Donna Michaels

~HC Heroes Series~
(Harland County Spinoff Series)

Mac
Carter (6/11/19)
Dex (9/2019)

~Harland County Series~

Harland County Christmas (Prequel)
Her Fated Cowboy
Her Unbridled Cowboy
Her Uniform Cowboy
Her Forever Cowboy
Her Healing Cowboy
Her Volunteer Cowboy
Her Indulgent Cowboy
Her Hell Yeah Cowboy
Her Troubled Cowboy (Citizen Soldier Crossover)
Her Hell No Cowboy
Her Doggone Cowboy
Harland County Epilogue

~The Citizen Soldier Series~
(Harland County Spinoff Series)

Wyne and Dine
Wyne and Chocolate
Wyne and Song
Wine and Her New Year Cowboy
Whine and Rescue
Wine and Hot Shoes
Wine and Scenery

~The Men of At Ease Ranch Series~
~Entangled Publications~

In An Army Ranger's Arms
Her Secret Army Ranger
The Right Army Ranger
Army Ranger with Benefits
The Army Ranger's Surprise

~Related~

Cowboy-Fiancé (formerly Cowboy-Sexy) (Hand drawn Japanese
Translation)
Cowboy Payback (sequel)

~Novels~

She Does Know Jack
Royally Unleashed
The Spy Who Fanged Me

DonnaMichaelsAuthor.com

ABOUT THE AUTHOR

Donna Michaels is an award winning, *New York Times & USA Today* bestselling author of *Romaginative* fiction. Her hot, humorous, and heartwarming stories include cowboys, men in uniform, and some sexy primal alphas who are equally matched by their heroines. With a husband recently retired from the military, a household of seven and several rescued cats, she never runs out of material. From short to epic, her books entertain readers across a variety of sub-genres, one was even hand-drawn into a Japanese translation...if only she could read it...

Bringing you HEAs-One Hot Alpha Hero at a Time

Thanks for reading,

~Donna

DonnaMichaelsAuthor.com

Made in the USA
Middletown, DE
21 September 2019